powerless

Also by Tim Dlugos

High There (Some of Us Press, 1973)
For Years (Jawbone, 1977)
Je Suis Ein Americano (Little Caesar Press, 1979)
A Fast Life (Sherwood Press, 1982)
Entre Nous (Little Caesar Press, 1982)
Strong Place (Amethyst Press, 1992)

powerless

selected poems 1973-1990

tim dlugos

edited by david trinidad

introduction by dennis cooper

HIGH RISK
BOOKS

NEW YORK / LONDON

Library of Congress Catalog Card Number: 95–71064

First published in 1996 by Serpent's Tail,
4 Blackstock Mews, London N4; and
180 Varick Street, 10th floor, New York, NY 10014

Cover design by Rex Ray
Set in 10pt Jansen by Intype London Ltd
Printed in Finland by Werner Söderström Oy

Acknowledgments

The poems in section one (except for "Desire Under the Pines") appeared in *Entre Nous* (Little Caesar Press, 1982).

"Desire Under the Pines" and the poems in section two (except for "Here Comes the Bride") appeared in *Strong Place* (Amethyst Press, 1992).

"Here Comes the Bride" appeared in *St. Mark's Poetry Project Newsletter*.

The poems in section three originally appeared in the following publications:

Brooklyn Review: "Powerless"
BOMB: "Harmony in Red," "Ordinary Time," "Radiant Child"
Chemical Imbalance: "Signs of Madness"
Long Shot: "Parachute"
OutWeek: "D.O.A.," "Turandot"
The Paris Review: "G-9"
Poets for Life (Crown): "Retrovir"
Santa Monica Review: "All Souls Day"
Shiny: "Etiquette in 1969"
Washington Review: "Swede"

For Christopher Wiss

Contents

Introduction   xi
Editor's Note   xv

1973–1981
Poem After Dinner   3
So Far   4
American Baseball   5
Gilligan's Island   6
Great Art   9
Stanzas for Martina   10
Great Books of the 1950s   14
At the Point   16
Day for Paul   17
You Are There   18
Note to Michael   20
"Hello, I'm Johnny Cash"   21
Bindo Altoviti   22
If I Were Bertolt Brecht   24
The Young Poet   25
Brian and Tim   27
Entre Nous   28
Pastorale   30
Qum   31
Chez Jane   32
East Longmeadow   34
Desire Under the Pines   37
The Lions of St. Mark's   38

1982–1986
On This Train Are People Who Resemble   45
Not Stravinsky   46
Summer, South Brooklyn   47
New Music   48
Psalm   49

To Walter Lowenfels   51
"Dear Heart, wish you or I were here or there . . ."   53
The Morning   55
Pretty Convincing   57
Spinner   60
The Fruit Streets   61
Healing the World From Battery Park   63
July   67
Here Comes the Bride   70

1988–1990
Retrovir   73
Ordinary Time   74
Signs of Madness   77
All Souls' Day   79
Parable   80
Powerless   81
G-9   84
Harmony in Red   102
Etiquette in 1969   104
Radiant Child   105
Swede   106
Parachute   109
Turandot   112
D.O.A.   113

Introduction

If not for the peculiar shape of the poetry world, Tim Dlugos would be major. He had the misfortune of being an original at a time when the poetry audience was dividing into camps, each of which expected poets to fulfill a particular role and nothing more. Tim, who was always and only true to his own personal sense of grace, didn't quite fit in. He was neither an identity-obsessed gay poet, a spoken word poet, an academic, nor a L=A=N=G=U=A=G=E poet. If Tim can be categorized at all, it's as a post-New York School poet, as he was deeply influenced by Ashbery, O'Hara, Schuyler, Elmslie and Koch, and counted among his friends other New York School offspring like Brad Gooch, Eileen Myles, Douglas Crase, John Yau, Alice Notley, and Joe Brainard.

Tim was a charismatic, generous, and yet elusive man who fraternized with an extraordinary range of creative people — painters, poets, novelists, rock stars, actors, models, fashion designers. His work reflects his ravenous fascination with the innumerable ways in which grace could be represented through artfulness. To those of us who knew him, and had our lives and work significantly altered by his sensibility both on and off the page, he was a bit like Frank O'Hara or Oscar Wilde must have been to earlier generations. To be his friend was to be guided through otherwise inaccessible, and in some cases seemingly conflicting worlds. One was always trailing after Tim as he flew between cocktail parties, poetry readings, art openings, the baths, services at his local church, and elsewhere, often over the course of a single evening. When he wasn't around, one traded stories about him. He was a star in a way poets almost never are. In fact if there was ever an artist who deserves an oral biography, it's Tim, both because his rather glamorous life was a fascinating thing in and of itself, and because any study of his fluid, complex life would also illuminate the heady artistic culture of the early 80s. Here's hoping some industrious biographer-type takes on the task before too many more of his contemporaries are dead.

I was lucky enough to meet Tim in the late 70s, thanks, if memory serves, to an introduction by the poet Michael Lally, who was one of Tim's mentors. At the time I was running a literary magazine and publishing house out of Los Angeles called Little Caesar, and I wound up issuing two of Tim's books, *Je Suis Ein Americano* (1979) and *Entre Nous* (1982). Tim and I became fast friends, and he began making frequent trips to Los Angeles to visit and do readings at the Beyond Baroque Literary/Arts Center where I was programming events. He quickly became a hero and inspiration to a group of young writers who hung around the Center, and which included Amy Gerstler, Benjamin Weissman, David Trinidad, Michael Silverblatt, Ed Smith, Kim Rosenfield, Jack Skelley and others. Through Tim's generosity and fantastic organizational instincts, a kind of Transcontinental scene of young writers formed, linking us on the West Coast with Tim's friends and colleagues on the East Coast, who included Myles, Gooch, Bernard Welt, Donald Britton, Cheri Fein, Steve Hamilton, and many others. Without this mutual support system, it would have been far more difficult for those of us in then-provincial Los Angeles to pursue our writing with real seriousness. And without Tim, it would have never happened.

Tim's work went through roughly four phases. His early poetry is clever, gentle, infused with a melancholic longing for ideal romance, and full of carefully attenuated horniness, often structured around and set in contrast to the fake perfect emotional lives of the TV sitcom characters with whom he grew up. The second phase sees his work becoming more physically enigmatic and complicatedly lyrical. His characteristic wit is more subtle and continuous, and the punch lines he favored early on are diffused into recurring fragments or interludes of an ongoing, pervasive joke far more scary and cosmic.

In the third and perhaps weakest phase of his work, which

paralleled a period of heavy drinking and on and off depression in his personal life, the poems become overly dense with word games and references to pop cultural icons. Tim always made showing off seem like an act of genius, but this work, while physically impressive, is slightly over-achieving in places. The poems' emotions seem scattered and impersonal, and there is the feeling that Tim is trying too hard to write a masterpiece. It was during this period that Tim wound up having something of a nervous collapse. He quit drinking, eliminated most of his social life, decided to become an Episcopal priest, reenrolled in school, left New York, and wrote very little poetry for a time.

The last phase of his writing, which paralleled his testing positive for the HIV virus and finding the first stable love relationship of his life, is maybe the strongest. These late poems are the simplest, most graceful, and most emotionally direct of all his works. They include the extraordinary and celebrated long poem "G-9," easily one of the most eloquent and moving poems to be written about the impact of the AIDS epidemic.

If there are such things as karma and justice, Tim Dlugos's work will outlast the trends and secure a place in the so-called canon if for no other reason than for the brilliant, complete, unique, and sometimes sublime pleasure it affords. I count myself among the many writers whose work was profoundly influenced by Tim's poetry. Thanks to the efforts of Ira Silverberg, Christopher Wiss, and David Trinidad, his wondrous achievement has the shot at immortality that he and it so richly deserve.

Dennis Cooper

Editor's Note

When Tim Dlugos died of AIDS in 1990, it had been almost ten years since *Entre Nous*, a book that includes poems he wrote between 1973 and 1981, was published. In the mid-eighties, he put together and attempted to publish a collection entitled *Strong Place*; there were no takers at that time. Shortly before his death, he revised the *Strong Place* manuscript. He also compiled his last poems into a manuscript called *Powerless*.

In 1992, I was a consulting editor to Amethyst Press, where I was able to see *Strong Place* into print. That house, unfortunately, went under soon afterwards and the book was never properly distributed. Efforts were also made to place *Powerless* with a large publisher. As accomplished and moving as Tim's writing is, it was impossible to establish the work of a dead poet in that commercial context. Consequently, it

was decided by Tim's lover and executor Christopher Wiss, Ira Silverberg, and myself that it would better serve Tim's work to publish a selected poems rather than continuing to seek a publisher for another single volume. It was further decided that the selected poems should also be called *Powerless*, as a way of honoring both the essence of Tim's later work and his own choice of title.

Tim asked me on his deathbed to look after his work, a task I unquestioningly accepted and one that's provided many moments of heartfelt satisfaction. Editing *Powerless* put me back in touch with poems that, years before, had influenced my own aesthetic; I wanted my writing to be as effervescent, offhanded, candid, and "real" as Tim's. Arranged chronologically, his poems easily fell into three sections: work from the books Tim published while he was alive, the *Strong Place* poems, and that final batch informed by his stunning near-death clarity. These sections can be seen as phases in Tim's artistic output, distinct periods of productivity.

My only regret is that it wasn't practical to include "A Fast

Life," Tim's marvelous thirty-part poem about coming out in the early seventies. The sequence would have fallen in the middle of the first section, and would have interrupted the continuity. I published "A Fast Life" as a Sherwood Press chapbook in 1982; it quickly disappeared and has been out of print since. It was Tim's first masterpiece: a generous account of a young poet's spiritual, sexual, and creative development. Perhaps one day this piece will be available again.

I would like to thank Christopher Wiss for his patience and understanding, Dennis Cooper for his editorial suggestions, and Ira Silverberg for making this book possible.

David Trinidad
New York City
January 1996

powerless

1973–1981

Poem After Dinner
for Tim

some things never run out:
my poverty, for instance,
is never exhausted
sandwiches for dinner again

your blond hair, for instance,
even if we're both exhausted
soothes me when we go outside
you and the forsythias

I get so excited
I think I'll read the Susan Sontag article
in *Partisan Review*
I want to walk beside you in the drizzle

and say you can move in with me
tonight, right away, even though
this time they'll probably evict me
and although I'm moving out in three weeks anyway

So Far

Saturday, Jan. 12: sky full

of clouds and the sun behind them
"intermittent" "hard-edged"

                        that's not unusual

go to sleep 5:30 after Heavy Talk w/ Joe
but that was Last Night, even though
the date is the same

                  I don't like remembering
Last Night when I wake with achy legs from
too much beer   so put Joni Mitchell on
(Morning Morgantown)   then switch to Bacall
in Applause as perhaps more appropriate

books for the afternoon: Dreaming As One
by Lewis Warsh and Stupid Rabbits by Michael Lally
also the new Art News, but that's a magazine

it's all about New Mexico! I wanted to ush
all summer at the Santa Fe Opera, but never
got west of Leesburg, Va.

                      unlike Belinda
                      unlike Chuck

some of the people I know live in California
others are talking outside my room   but
everyone, no matter how far the physical distance
is only a phone call away

I am happy when I remember that

American Baseball

It's for real, not for practice, and it's televised,
not secret, the way you'd expect a civilized country
to handle delicate things, it's in color, it's happening
now in Florida, 'This Is American Baseball' the announcer
announces as the batter enters the box, we are watching,
and it could be either of us

           standing there waiting
for the pitch, avoiding the eye of the pitcher as we take
a few practice cuts, turning to him and his tiny friends in
the outfield, facing the situation, knowing that someone
behind our backs is making terrible gestures, standing
there to swing and miss

           the way I miss you, wanting to be out   5
of uniform, out of breath, in your car, in love again, learning
all the signals for the first time, the way we learned the rules
of night baseball as high school freshmen: first base, you kiss
her, second base, her breasts, third, you're in her pants, and
home is where the heart

           wants to be all the time, but seldom
can reach past the obstacle course of space, the home in our
perfect future we wanted so badly, and want more than ever since
we learned we won't live there, which happens to lovers in civilized
countries all the time, and happens too in American baseball when
you strike out and remember what the game really meant.

Gilligan's Island

The Professor and Ginger are standing in the space in front
of the Skipper's cabin. The Professor is wearing deck shoes,
brushed denim jeans, and a white shirt open at the throat.
Ginger is wearing spike heels, false eyelashes, and a white
satin kimono. The Professor looks at her with veiled lust
in his eyes. He raises an articulate eyebrow and addresses
her as Cio-Cio-San. Ginger blanches and falls on her knife.

* * *

Meanwhile it is raining in northern California. In a tiny
village on the coast, Rod Taylor and Tippi Hedren are totally
concerned. They realize that something terrible is happening.
Each has been savagely attacked by a wild songbird within
the last twenty-four hours. Outside their window thousands
of birds have gathered in anticipation of the famous school-
yard scene. Tippi Hedren is wearing a colorful lipstick.

* * *

Ginger stares back at the Professor. His sullen good looks
are the perfect foil for her radiant smile. The Skipper and
Gilligan come into sight. The Skipper has been chasing
Gilligan around the lagoon for a long time now. Gilligan
holds onto his hat in the stupid way he has of doing things
like that. The Professor's lips part in a sneer of perfect
contempt. Ginger bares her teeth, as if in appreciation.

* * *

Jackie Kennedy bares her teeth. Behind and above her, the muzzle of a high-powered rifle protrudes from a window. A little man is aiming at Jackie Kennedy's husband. The man is wearing bluejeans and a white T-shirt. There isn't a bird to be seen. As he squeezes the trigger, the little man mutters between clenched teeth, "Certs is a candy mint." The hands of Jackie Kennedy's husband jerk automatically toward his head.

* * *

The Professor is noticing Ginger's breasts. He thinks of the wife he left at home, who probably thinks he's dead. He thinks of his mother, and all of the women he has ever known. Mr. and Mrs. Howell are asleep in their hut, secure in their little lives as character actors. Ginger shifts her weight to the other foot. The intensity of the moment reminds the Professor of a Japanese city before the end of the war.

7

* * *

In his mind he goes down each aisle in his government class, focusing on each face, each body. He is lying on his bed with his white shirt off and his trousers open. Dorothy Kirsten's voice fills the room. He settles on a boy who sits two desks behind him. He begins to masturbate, his body moving in time with the sad music. At moments like these he feels farthest away. As he shoots, his lips part and he bares his teeth.

* * *

The Professor and Ginger are watching each other across the narrow space. The Skipper and Gilligan have disappeared down the beach. The Howells are quietly snoring. The Professor and Ginger are alone. From the woods comes the sound of strange birds. From the water comes a thick and eerie tropical silence. The famous conversation scene is about to start. Clouds appear in the sky, and it begins to snow.

Great Art
for Donald Grace

Underneath your skin, your heart
moves. Your chest
rises at its touch. A small bump
appears, every
second. We watch for what appears
to be hours.

Our hands log the time: the soft
light, darkness
underneath your eyes. Our bodies
intersect like highways
with limitless access and perfect spans
of attention.

We pay for this later. I pay
for breakfast. We
can't stay long. We take off
to the museum
and watch the individual colors
as they surface

in the late works of Matisse.
They move the way
your heart moves, the way we breathe.
You draw your own
breath, then I draw mine. This is
truly great art.

Stanzas for Martina

1.

One minute you can be in
Baltimore, the next minute
you can be in Africa, riding
in the largest desert in the
world, on a bus 2 years ago:
that is nothing new

                    or even
interesting, Proust pushed it
so far into my consciousness
it's part of how I see things
every day, the way daily mass
used to be, or masturbation

I tell you this because I
called your office 5 minutes
ago and they said you Weren't There

2.

Smog alert. Way to head off
nuclear arms race. Beiderbecke.
Strange summer of '74.

New Ulster blueprint. Variety
of lifestyles. Separatist feelings.
Who ordered posters torn down?

Youths beat path to farm again.
Watergate wrongs didn't work.
America's great old resort hotels.
A century of Charles Ives.

Big wheels and deals.
Haiku-like perceptions.
Peek at a glittering age.
The older brother I never knew.

3.

These are the places I would
like to live: Santa Fe, New York,
Paris, N. Brookfield, Mesopotamia
Ohio (but not for too long), Florence,
Tangier, Mexico City,

                    Provincetown
(off-season), Cuernavaca, Manchester
Vt. (I spent about 5 hours doing this
with Joe O'Hare in 1969, we turned our
deepest desires loose over 5 continents

& ended up back in the stairwell of
College Hall, sitting out an ice storm
the year we were depressed by Philadelphia),
the settings of my favorite novels

4.

I am hoping that these stanzas
will have a cumulative effect.
I am vaguely annoyed by the classic
sound of "a"s at the ends of words.
I deplore melodrama. I suspect
charisma. I am wary of change

in my living situation. Meanwhile
the sky is dark where it hits
the Post Office tower: years of accumulated

grime. I don't know if the clock works.
Twelve stories up you can feel the damp
of subway excavation, see the damp
good looks of the workers. No
revolution without them, please.

5.

Half of the flags are at halfmast.
The others are all the way up.
This indicates the death of
a moderately famous person.

I can't touch people I don't really know.
I mean, can't really touch them.
This is not an exclusively Catholic issue.

I want to be tough.
Okay, everyone has problems.
Life is hard, and most of us
have lots more to go through.

One smile on the street, though,
& I take off. The sun can be
so strong it makes your head ache.

6.

Each time you reach a clearing you see
bears, like the same bear, over & over:
the look of surprise, the discontent.
Next to the road, 2 boys lie face down,
very still. They've been there a long time;
now they are perceived as landmarks, and books
have been written to explain their mysterious
pose. Above the woods the view is dim. When

you stop the car, your dept. chairman frolics
in the snow like an otter facing extinction.

You are afraid to go near the ravine.
You don't want to fall.
You suddenly understand why you are there.
A powerful sadness takes total control of your life.

7.

Midnight. Wake up (sleeping
since sunset). Don't turn
lamp on (Randy asleep).
Pad around apt. in search
of glasses. Thinking how much
tougher Alice Notley can be
than Bernadette Mayer, for instance.
Oranges green under kitchen light;
subject of important experiments.
Dick Powell movie on TV, followed
by Judy Holliday. They're both dead.

Want to call you up & say
Hi, the houseguests never arrived
& we didn't go out after all.

Great Books of the 1950s

I Was A Communist For The FBI

You have joined the Communist Party to give inside information
to the FBI. No one is aware that you are really a loyal American.
Your mother dies thinking you're a Communist. Your younger
brother beats you up. Even when the Communists kill your
girlfriend, you can't do a thing. Finally you testify before
a Congressional committee and triumphantly watch the faces
of the Communist leaders as you expose their secret plans.

The Old Man And The Sea

You write a symbolic novel about the eternal struggle between
the wills of strong men and the forces of nature. You select
a baseball star to function as a hero for two Spanish-surnamed
males. But they're the real heroes. You envision Spencer
Tracy in the movie version of your novel, and are totally
delighted when you learn that the Hollywood moguls have
picked him for the part.

Black Like Me

You want to know what it is like to be black, so you dye your
skin and head south. You have many strange experiences, several
of which are sexual in nature and involve sadistic white men.
When you tire of this, you drive home and write a book describing
your travels. The book shocks and enrages the white community,
and vaguely embarrasses Negro leaders. By the time your skin
returns to its original color, you have got a best seller on your
hands.

Profiles In Courage

During your recovery from a war-related injury, you collect information about members of the U.S. Senate who destroyed their political careers rather than abandon their principles. You find eight such men, and write a book about their fortitude. The year the book is published, you decide to run for President yourself. The magic returns to your marriage.

At the Point

It is after midnight. Your fat friend
decides to go swimming. He takes off
all his clothes. The headlights of a car
flash, illuminate his body as he moves
down the road toward the beach.

The boy you are in love with lights
a joint. You are both at the end
of the boardwalk. Smoke rises into
the intense blue sky from his mouth.
His papers are covered with stars.

You actually ache with the desire to
touch the man in bed beside you. He is
on the college faculty, you are one of
his brightest students. It takes you
a long time to get back to sleep.

There are two houses. The big one is filled
with your friends who are going away.
There is a piano in the tiny house. You
walk into the empty parlor, sit down, and
play the only song you know by heart.

Day for Paul

Home for lunch. Find bright light smeared on furniture
like red shoe polish. This happens every day when I'm
not here. Strength of sun through window makes me dizzy;
I can't eat cheese, drink milk or beer. Run hands beneath
cool water and wash my eyes. Check comics: Dagwood hangs
onto streetcar with both hands, moves down hill toward work
at high speed. He lives in one of the cities I love: San
Francisco, Boston, and one other. I live in political
capital, sniff out trouble spots. Smoke across the river
in another state. Boy with wire-rimmed glasses and moustache
smokes a joint in parents' house. Everybody else is asleep.
He lights up

        the sky is pink near horizon up hill from
tomb of unknown soldier, then turns brown as eyes travel
to the level of the roof across alley, it fades into soft
white, like fluorescent tube in gray room, then moves out
of sight above the line where window slips back into wall.
I don't move forward. I sit perfectly still. The only sound
in room is nib of pen as it moves across paper

                        it's me
five years ago. I am on the verge of big breakthrough
accompanied by pain. I have not read anything by Proust,
Dostoevsky, Rimbaud, or Frank O'Hara. I have not had sex
with the people I love and need most. I have not yet learned
to identify the people I love and need most. But I have
dreams about people who move like you, who make me feel so
full that waking up becomes a major letdown, and I want to
sleep all day and all night if it will make me feel that good
again, take me to the place inside my body where I can feel
you living all the time.

You Are There

Wake to rain when phone rings, it's a man I went to bed with in another city, says parade was cancelled again. New year. Knives in throat from smoking dope for first time in a year at party last night. Smoke dope in Terry's apartment, listen: just because it's Dylan taking me out again doesn't mean that things can be the same. Oh no. Cry of tiny man who opens door to tiny room in my heart after a long vacation. The dust clears and the light is steady. Don't take this seriously.

You make me feel brand new. I watch you get fucked up, lose touch: you're gentle and you're beautiful, it's 1972. It's 1973 and I pick you up in a bookstore for ride home; you have to buy a scarf in Georgetown. Freezing day. I didn't mean to put this down so soon, I wanted to lead up to it, take the streetcar to the top of the hill, coast down to the intersection. Still too bad, too serious. It's tough they only give respect to straight-looking men. It's New Years in the little luncheonette.

I want you to know how fine you looked. I tell you things I haven't told anyone else. I am in your bedroom, I am learning to write. You open your   the photograph collection of your past can be limitless; the process is to slice each section of your history thinner and thinner until you are left with one fraction of a moment so clear — the raindrop halfway down the pane — that you can live through it again, so perfect in detail that you can watch your image breathe. Love and death meet here. Click of slide tray on the carousel. Love and death meet here.

Shine light through situation and the colors aren't right, like my father's first attempts in basement darkroom. Koda-color, 1954: toddler under arbor in the public park, facing bright green flowers. I never talked to flowers the way Ted Green-wald can. On mescaline in 1970, I understood the trees for the first time, still do. The clumsiness of love, the slow awareness of where the roots are, of what the roots absorb. Naked hand palm up in air, no breeze. The sun bombards your skin with energy.

You are there, and the announcer with sad eyes, holding back the excitement in his voice, tells you You Are There, but the reinforcing wall inside his throat is too weak, his voice cracks and the pure excitement surges up into the hatchway of his face, the mouth, past white teeth in one strong current, straining toward the outer world it overflows into, coloring the waves of sound that break upon the ears of millions with the colors of the manic and totally new. And it is our history, yours and mine, that draws this out, that causes such a pressure in the throat of the man with sad eyes.

Note to Michael

strange to see the river through the window
that lets the colors in behind me   it's real light
as opposed to artificial   it's real life
I'm in the middle of, I hope   where you are
is just as real (I also hope)   and
what we feel between us is a filament that bears
its own energy, glowing in ways too subtle
or too fast for the eye to pick up, a precious alloy
that puts us in the same place "on one level":
the level of the river and the light

Hello, I'm Johnny Cash,
inventor of the first pay toilet,
the Johnny-Cash, which isn't my real name
at all, but the name of my original product.
I took it as my own when the powers-that-be
stole my great idea and made a killing.
They're sneaky bastards, the powers-that-be.
They're the guys who run things.
The President and all the heroes work for them,
and so did I.
They're the guys who make the wars,
who own the gold and land.
They're the ones who'll say this monologue
"sounds like a warmed-over Blitzstein libretto"
in the *Times* tomorrow. But I don't care
anymore, if I can sing my songs.

I wrote them all
myself. They're mostly about things
that I remember and people I knew.
I'm fortunate enough to have been personally present
at many historic scenes.
I was there when Judith Crist had her moments of doubt and pain.
I wrote a song, "Who Killed the Kennedys,"
and made a killing when it went gold.
And I was a guest on the old *Tonight* show
the night Jack Paar stormed off because the powers-
that-be
scotched his famous reference to a certain "W.C."
They thought he was exposing how they purloined my invention,
when he merely was saying a secret hello
to his favorite poet in Rutherford, N.J.

This next song's going out to my favorite poet.
So the powers-that-be remain in the dark,
I won't use your initials, but
you live in New York, and you know who you are.

Bindo Altoviti

Bindo Altoviti walks into the back yard letting the screen door slam. He slings his lanky torso into a webbed chair and pops a can of Miller High Life Beer. It's the champagne of bottled beers, the perfect drink to quench the thirst of a boy as effervescent as Bindo. The light in Bindo's eyes helps him see. He picks up Section C of the *Times* (*Sports Monday*) and idly scans the pages. He is looking for a picture of a man in whom the brilliant light that Bindo knows from personal experience has been captured and transformed into tensile strength. Long legs. Long afternoon. Bindo stretches, dances to avoid a pesky bee. He lights a skinny joint and settles back to get high. The world is like a big museum to Bindo and he's no famous artist. He's just a kid with long hands pinned against a white wall he doesn't know enough to call by its right name.

On campus, Bindo wears a purple smock. It covers his tight jeans. He wants people to like him for himself, not because he turns them on. He's an eccentric figure as he walks across the quad, his floppy garment a flag of revolution in a world of letter sweaters and alligator shirts. Bindo doesn't paint, he gets painted, and he sees that as a major difference between himself and the pustulated masses grubbing for advanced degrees. He separates himself from their tiny world by degrees: hoagies in bed instead of feeding at the common trough. But Bindo is too nice a person to remain aloof for long. He lazes in the grove of Academe, and feeds its wildest birds by hand.

What Bindo needs is someone to bring him out of himself, or, what Bindo needs is someone to force him to stay the same, keep him from moving, handcuff him to a metal frame and never let him go, grow, grow old, graduate. Gradually

Bindo distills a plan. It's still inside the big room, cooled by the world's first air-conditioner that doesn't hum.

A painting is a window. Bindo looks inside. It's boring. Something deep inside him is boring its way to the surface. He leans against the marble columns with his thumbs hooked on his belt, waiting to see what will emerge. It's no emergency. It's an afternoon that lasts as long as you want it, sweet kid with a salty skin and long hands trying to be cool, air-conditioned building on a vaguely threatening street, muggy summer, strong and brilliant light.

If I Were Bertolt Brecht

I'd take a bath, first of all;
then I'd throw away those drab and ratty
suits I'm always photographed wearing.
Buy some new threads; and while I'm at it,
get myself in shape at the nearest Holiday
Health Spa. Next I'd trim the fat
off my plays, getting rid of the didactic
boring passages that make me such a German
artist. I'd develop a modest sense of humor
and a sense of modesty, and treat the ladies
better — they're people, too. If I hated
California as much as I say, I'd leave and go
somewhere I liked better; but I love California,
so that would eliminate a lot of grief.
I'd shave the silly moustache, get a tan,
and turn my life into a sane and happy one,
all before I went out for my sauerkraut
and knockwurst, into the Weimar night.

The Young Poet

for Dennis Cooper

The young poet's work is sharp, stylish, and oddly moving.

The young poet's novel-in-progress is being written in collaboration with a National Book Award winning older poet.

The young poet takes off his shirt and poses for a drawing by David Hockney.

The young poet spends some time in L.A.

The young poet was Allen Ginsberg's secretary for a month.

The young poet cannot help that he is handsome enough to model.

The young poet got propositioned by Donald Barthelme in 1974.

The young poet goes to the Duchess and gets drunk.

The young poet goes to a gym and mounts a Nautilus.

The young poet buys an electric guitar, and dreams in Tier 3.

The young poet works in an office.

The young poet learns to rejoice that she is pregnant.

The young poet marries another young poet.

The young poets give their offspring unusual first names.

The young poet has bad teeth.

The young poet shops at Reminiscence.

The young poet lives on the Lower East Side.

The young poet applies for food stamps.

The young poet applies for a National Endowment grant.

The young poet applies for a job in a famous bookstore.

The young poet is a blatant imitator of Ashbery.

The young poet walks like Ted Berrigan.

The young poet used to flirt with Anne Waldman.

The young poet writes reviews.

The young poet stuffs envelopes at St. Mark's.

The young poet wonders if it's time for a haircut.

The young poet wears black.

The young poet knows the distinction between punk and New Wave.

The young poet sees the book as object.

The young poet is unabashedly ambitious.

The young poet starts to write fiction as a way of opening her
  language up.
The young poet changes her name to something more perky.
The young poet doesn't ask for autographs.
The young poet is a junkie.
The young poet is a fag.
The young poet is a cheerfully middle-class suburbanite set down
  in the middle of a self-consciously bohemian scene.
The young poet is a lush.
The young poet has a small press.
The young poet got published once in *Partisan Review*.
The young poet wants more than anything to have the first book
  published by Angel Hair, Viking, Z Press, Black Sparrow,
  or Lita Hornick's Kulchur Press.
The young poet gets quietly drunk at Lita Hornick's parties.
The young poet gets loudly drunk at Lita Hornick's parties and
  is asked to leave.
The young poet affects an English accent.
The young poet affects an Oriental religion.
The young poet drinks European beer.
The young poet deals grass.
The young poet is doomed by his career as an arts administrator.
The young poet studied under Kenneth Koch.
The young poet voted for Ed Koch.
The young poet takes himself or herself exceptionally seriously.
The young poet gets a little older, and his poetry matures.

Brian and Tim

New York	Massachusetts
D.C.	New York
the mountains	the ocean
St. Bonny's	LaSalle
graduate degree	college dropout
ceramics	poetry
Paris	Dakar
Denver	L.A.
Chinese	French
ex-Catholic	bad Catholic
waiter	copywriter
Rehoboth Beach	Fire Island Pines
bridge	TV
Montaigne	Frank O'Hara
Rascals	The Ninth Circle
sleeping with someone	sleeping alone
going home with someone on the second date	going home with someone on the first meeting
introducing self before having sex	having sex before introducing self
young men	boys
The Dry Look	The Wet Look
Moet	Heineken
a townhouse	a highrise
red	blue
twenty-eight	thirty-one
twenty-six	twenty
ratatouille	paella
an altar boy	a priest
A Confederacy of Dunces	*Our Mutual Friend*
conservative Republican	Sixties liberal
Jockey briefs	boxer shorts
overwork	indolence
psilocybin	mescaline
cocaine	cocaine
Lacoste	Lacoste
Proust	Proust

Entre Nous

I took a lot of guff about the team I coached
the intramural freshmen, entre nous
between the walls, not off them
sealing off their fate beneath a roof
of stars, sports illustrated
as in comic parodies of shooting hoops
a good day, shot a hundred (sky
darkened by the endless flocks of passenger
pigeons, children aim their 22s anywhere,
horizon to horizon)   it was the final season and
I took a lot of flak about the jackets we wore
me and the boys, we'd put on our jackets
and go out shooting, wild game, a game
of our invention   fouled out by the bum
of a referee, bummed out by the atmosphere
(invisible)   but buoyed up by the cheers
from the darkness just beyond the floodlights
that flooded our awareness with our fate
* YOU ARE LOVED *   I took a lot of pains
to get here, only to find myself a pigeon
a passenger on some fool's train
of jerkoff thoughts and blind desire   I broke
a finger when the ball was passed to me, and broke up,
flubbing the shot   but cheered up by the boy's
intensity, I lightened my burden as I lighted up
the joint and its dark atmosphere   I took a deep breath
of relief, and plunged back into the fray
my collar and my nerves were fraying, till
you came along, and opened up the floodgates
in my chest, the irrigation pumps
that fertilize the acreage entre nous
an empty space we've slated for development
which small birds you released fly over on their way
to nowhere   I fly across the floodplain

in a Piper Cub, on my way to the horizon
a cub scout to your pied piper, straight into
the endless Alp's dark atmosphere
I took a vow that when the door swung open
I'd enter to a choral * YOU ARE LOVED *
but broke the vow and headed through the ceiling,
sealing off my fantasies and breathing in
an atmosphere the stars of my invention never
punctuate, far beyond the pinspots,
buoyed up by a dense awareness that I am
a passenger shooting through my personal experience
on the way to Destination: Entre Nous
a famous space I still believe exists

Pastorale

for Virgil Moore

The time the toddler crapped on the Urban Center floor
and we left it for the janitors to handle
you said it was a statement of the building's true
significance to the community; that, or just laughed.
Now you're dead five years, and I'm wondering
what you'd say was the significance of your presence
to those you "touched forever" (you'd laugh at that,
too). Update: Mary Ellen is a therapist in Center
City. John is a professional actor (so what else
is new, you'd say), Jack is married, Kevin
is divorced. I'm a writer living in New York.
Caught the upward mobility escalator
and live in a renovated building with a view
of the harbor, cheek-by-jowl with the poor
whose lives we thought would have improved by now
through self-determination and a brand new kind
of socialism, one which put down nobody.

I'm looking out the window at the water and the ships,
thinking of all you've missed. Reagan got elected
President! You shake with silent laughter and your eyes
are full of instant knowledge. *Right*, you'd say.
A few clouds hang against the blue; the water's patchy
where they block the light. You tried to swim at night,
you who were so frightened by the water, and went down
trying. Sometimes from this vantage point
it's 1960 again, the air can be so clear
it's like a dream of lost time, before the dope,
before the lost revolution. Your silence is as much a sign
as ever when I think of your laughter and the way you left:
going out by getting high and doing something impossible.

Qum
for Donald Britton

Saturday, Jan. 12: sky swarms
with microscopic particles. It's too warm
inside this bar, a grace note
to make you and my other friends assume I wrote
these words just now, before the reading.
That is an illusion. Needing
drastic forms of admiration is a virus.
Wanting people to desire us
we (meaning you and I) wear a bright veil
of language (meaning words) before which pale
the mundane elements of waking life.
"A poet." Fine. But sometimes I feel like the wife
of a demented mullah, in my thick chador,
two eyes peeping out, no body curves or
smile or sense of pity.
Marching through the streets of this holy city,
I can smell the slogans on my breath,
and my veil is Western journalism's symbol of the death
of reason and the triumph of some crazy throwback
to my suburban Moslem childhood. I can't go back
there any more. The keys won't
fit. Sometimes I don't
remember that this holy garb was of my choosing:
brilliant blue, like Mary's. God, I'm losing
my train of thought, awash in archetypal sentiment.
The words are microscopic particles, a sediment
of mirrored light, brilliant, filling the air
and piling up around us layer by layer.

Chez Jane

"I think it's fun to go to the prom
with a girl. I liked it." Your head
is in the clouds, like the observation deck
of the World Trade Center, and the clouds
are gray. "You know, you really look
like a woman." I'm writing off the top
of my head in your loft with its tropical
appointments: Cayo Hueso shorts, droopy
potted palms, complicated hash pipe
from Honduras, and a bright though eerie
bird perched on the petal of a huge
white orchid in your painting, the one
I admire. All this sounds "outlandish"
like the movie I hate, but it's not: it belongs
and illuminates, as unexpected and exotic
as the sailboat moored outside your window,
thirty feet offshore with people on its deck
and no way they could possibly have gotten there,
as if a mundane obstacle like transportation
had miraculously been solved, the way it's done
in movies: cut to the glamorous
soiree, and let the viewers fill in the intervening
action on their own. It's nice to drift through the history
of film within your view: a great ape
scaling the twin towers, Jessica Lange in tow;
Al Pacino swaggering in leather and chains,
four blocks to the south; and Laura Mars ensconced
in *New York Magazine*'s idea of luxury
where gay men sunbathe nude along the rotten
pier. But it can be just as swell to simply
follow the horizon with your eyes, the skyline
complicated, unfamiliar, from Bedloe's
(now known as Liberty) Island, past Hoboken
and the great green docks, up to where the giant cup

of Maxwell House is yielding its last drop. It's good
to have this vantage point, to fill in the river's
graduated silvers with your eyes, and watch the gray
of sky and street diverge to gold and misty blue,
like the eyes of a mariner. "I feel like one, too."

East Longmeadow

Endicott Peabody was the governor.

Dick Hickey, Jerry Pellegrini and Frederick Wheeler were the selectmen.

Richard Clark was the town clerk.

Father John Wolohan was the parish priest.

Clyde Walb was the scoutmaster.

Donald Emerson (blond, crewcut) was the sixth-grade teacher.

Officer Craven was the police sergeant.

Miss Eseldra Glynn was the other sixth-grade teacher.

Mr. Francis was the only Negro teacher.

James Latourelle was the plumber and Little League manager.

John Quinn was the doctor.

James Brown was the dentist.

Robert Bean was the grocer.

Sanford Nooney owned the hardware store.

Ed Pratt ran the Esso station.

Frank O'Hearn was the real estate agent.

W. Harley Rudkin wrote the humor column for the *Sunday Republican*.

Stuart Crapser was the principal of Birchland Park Junior High School.

Angelo Correale ("Gorilla") was the assistant principal of Birchland Park Junior High School.

Kenneth Battige was the leader of the hoods.

The Brega twins were the wild kids on the street.

Father Hugh Crean was the assistant parish priest.

Charles Bowler was the town Democratic chairman.

Helen Hayward was the town nurse.

Lois Lopes was the librarian.

Mrs. Jones, a Negro, was the Avon lady.

Alonzo "Dennis" Jones was the school basketball star.

Wescott Clarke (blond, crewcut) was the handsomest boy in school.

Nancy Dalessio was the prettiest girl in school.

John Quill was the TV weatherman.

William L. Putnam owned the TV station, WWLP.

Jimmy Fiore was the grocer for the Italians.

Walter Uhlman was the town engineer.

Hiram Moody was the town eccentric.

Mr. Teed was the Congregational minister.

Brian Crosby was retarded.

Mary Gregory was the president of the Catholic Women's Club.

Billy Barrett was the head altar boy.

Cookie Bates was the leader of a Dixieland band, and wore a goatee.

Ruth McMullen taught art, and wore a smock.

Allen Pash (blond, crewcut) was the boys' gym teacher.

Dorothy Gladden was the moderator of the Poetry Appreciation Club.

Laurie Richmond was the girl whose mother had shot her in her bed before committing suicide.

John Brusnicki was the pharmacist.

Vincent Panetta was the divorce lawyer.

Mrs. Blake was the richest woman in town.

Marion Cooley was the piano teacher.

William Twohig was the postmaster.

Archie Rintoul ran the Community Feed Store.

Fred Geoffrion Senior had a nervous tic he got in the war.

Helen Geoffrion was a practical nurse.

Harvey Cadwell was the guidance counselor.

Genevieve Crosby was the mother of three who introduced the sack dress to town.

Diane Johnson eloped at age 14 to Elkton, Maryland.

David Lyons had cerebral palsy.

Paul Ollari was the paper boy.

Jeanette Goodlatte wrote the "East Longmeadow News" column for the *Union*.

Wilton Hayes had a wooden leg.

Joe Siano was the barber.

Babe Meacham was known as "The Mayor of Maple Street."

Ann Dunbar owned the ladies clothing store.

Mrs. Baldwin ran the Busy Bee Kindergarten.

Raymond Drury was the disc jockey for WTYM, "*Time* for Beautiful Music."

Stephen Brega was brain-damaged after he tried to hang himself.

Elwin Doubleday was the high school principal.

Nora Braylee was the leader of Youth for Christ.

Jimmy Walb was the president of Demolay.

Fred Lindner was the man who sharpened lawnmower blades.

Dolores McDonald was Mary Gregory's sidekick.

Tom Williams was an executive at Package Machinery.

David Bowe had a speech impediment.

John Hird was president of the Harvard Club.

Howard Frykberg owned a restaurant on Route 20 that failed when the Turnpike opened.

Bob Latourelle was the captain of the Little League team.

36 Eddie Lombard was the milkman.

Robert Drumheller owned a German shepherd that always chased my bike.

Desire Under the Pines

I like to wake up early by myself
and walk out to the forest which divides
the beach from bay side of the island, like
the line of hair that starts at breastbone, hides

the navel and descends into the thatch
beneath the tan line of a boy I saw
a picture of once, in a magazine.
He isn't in the woods this morning. Raw

desire al fresco isn't quite my speed
these months. I like to scout for vireos
and robins almost as much as for guys.
An ashtray from the Hotel Timeo

in Taormina, a signed lithograph
by the late Tony Smith, and a shelf packed
with great books of our time: the souvenirs
of my hosts' histories. I left mine back

along the trail, like interesting litter
thrown out of Conestogas on the long
trek west. The drivers knew that "We can use it
in Oregon" was a completely wrong

criterion. They had to get there first,
and lightening the load was the only way.
Beside the path, the wren that lights in brush
sounds like a footstep in the gathering day.

The Lions of St. Mark's

for Edmund White

1.

It is partly a matter of light.
Mornings, one feels it gathering
the strength it needs to melt the unabsorbed
dew between the shoulder blades, from last
night's steam. The process
is guaranteed to be in satisfactory order
hours down the pike. There's time
to fill a few more reams before the map of Florida's
spread across a corner of Tar Beach, making us
honorary Sun People, though the clouds
and shadows that obscure the eyes of some
galoot are endlessly more magic.
Strange to think the pristine air controls
the somber damp that muffles all the bells
of the Basilica. In the little Polish
parish down the street, it's time
to light a candle, partly from devotion
but mostly for the image it provokes:
nostalgic you as supplicant, mantilla bobbing,
kneeling on the slab before a saint whose up-
turned eyes are hidden by a cloud of smoke.
He has been expunged from the calendar
like a wasted day, though we like to think
that no day's truly wasted. Rising late
and raising the venetian blinds, one quick glimpse
of sun in the piazza and the grazing herds
of pigeons marks the scene indelibly
as laundry. Then back to the rumpled sheets.
Later there'll be time to hit the Gem
Spa for Camels, but for now the wisps
of vapor left over from last night are
enough to make the well-tuned habit purr.
This is familiar music.

2.

The Venetians, till then under the care
of the obscure St. Theodore and his crocodile,
urgently needed the particular care
of some more eminent divine. They were weary
of the tennis shirts, mostly; alligator
tears over the death of style expressed in pastel
blousons, each emblazoned with the saint's
particular emblem: no dice. This street needed
scouring when the gentry moved in more, perhaps,
than in the unself-conscious days when Ukies
passed long hours strumming native instruments
on the stoops beneath a broiling sun, as pallid
in Hawaiian shirts and leis as ever in the hell-
hole of the kitchen at the Kiev. Arthur Godfrey's
voice trailed out the window like a string
of sputum waiting for some arriviste
to fall for the illusion of the light and try
to slip the pearls on one by one, scattering
the unself-conscious products of the Great South Bay
like so much litter. When the water
rises, the stones in the piazza
seem to be a crop of shellfish. It's why
they gave the lions wings — to fly away from here
and never get their feet wet. Slogging through
the Arsenal last night, we thought
they had the right idea.

3.

The arched bridge turns the canals into highways.
Let's take a ride in the speedboat!
There's no way to get lost; the Campanile's
calm demarcations of the light's
intensities will penetrate our lazy skulls
even in the panicky minutes when its mass is
hidden by the spray from other joycraft.
Did I tell you about my wonderful ride
down the Grand Canal with Peggy Guggenheim? We talked
about the literary lions, and I wish
that I could imitate the way she flew
from anecdote to anecdote. There was a terrific
story of Auden on his first acid trip. He walked
out to the street and saw the mailman smile
three blocks away. Apart from that, it was
a normal day. Post-nap, pre-tea: the normal
constitutional. She had her fluffy
dogs with her, and they sent up quite a row
when we sped under bridges where the cats
crowded the parapets. This is a metropolis
of cats. They lounge among the houseplants
in the windows of converted slums, the better
ones of which have Peggy Guggenheim's autobiography,
Out of This Century, on the coffee table next to Volume
One of the new Proust and the obligatory
crop of cat cartoons.

4.

When the Basilica was burnt, and the precious body lost,
a special miracle was devised, a form of replacement
borrowing the pagan notion of the soul's
migration. They found another body, looking
like the first. And the crowds rejoiced, sending
pigeons skyward. I had an identical dinner (chicken,
Pinot Grigio, and a salad with ambitious
dressing) last night in a place around the corner.
Mostly, I'm off beef; crowds of meaty
lookalikes have turned me from the whole
experience. They line up at the Saint's
front door as the lions glower and the lamps
snap on. There's something heady in his patronage
that made our city's troops invincible beneath
the pennant of a great evangelist. It's a team I'm proud
to have played on, but now I think there must be
more to life, although it's way too early
for fleshing out exactly what. Have a pastry
at a table in the colonnade. A fizzy drink
awaits you in its little red icebox.

5.

Sometimes in a brutal winter night, you may hear
the distant roar. And sometimes you may hear the slap
of hand on thigh that indicates a merry joke
among the mute, because you don't hear laughter.
Thank the stars tonight's not one of them.
You ramble past the dark cabanas on the Lido
and watch the lions sport in mid-air, under the last
full moon of a summer when the stifling wind
has kept its distance. This old slug-a-bed
wants a little fresh air to clear his head
before being swept away by sleep. The candle
in the lantern smokes too much, clouding
your eyes as water laps your Weejuns. A Parisian
novelist spent time here, kept a journal; and a German
liederdichter died here, partly from devotion
to an image that provoked. Mr. Lewes fell into the Grand
Canal, while Miss Evans and the other lions
roared. A land requiring sealegs is a dark
and perverse place, until the light comes back,
sending all the little mammals scurrying
and you across the street (barefoot, with trousers
rolled) to buy more cigarettes, this time
the Canadian brand with a Victorian
sailor on the packet. There should be a cathedral
of addiction on the corner where the bialy man
hangs out, full of shrines to the tobacco emblems
and Ah Men catalogs of yore, as well as to great
moments in the histories of Sun People: the first
trip to Florida, the birthday party
where you met the leading lights, the glint
at noon on lions' golden wings, and the Lido
afternoon when we whipped up a pitcher
of vodka and Campari and placed bets
on which would be the first to sink,
the city or the sun.

1982–1986

On This Train Are People Who Resemble

Allen Ginsberg
President Carter
Lynne Dreyer
Geraldine Fitzgerald
a monkey
Brian Epstein
Don Bachardy
the son on "Sanford and Son"
Rose Lesniak
Mrs. Sanders (neighbor, 1966)
Erin Clermont
Sid Caesar in drag
Terry Bartek (wrestling partner, high school gym class)
"Dad" on "Dennis the Menace" — in fact, I think it *is* Dad, "Henry
                              Mitchell," grayer and with deep
                              lines in his face but the same
                              receding chin and purse-mouthed but
                              benevolent expression, in a summer
                              suit that's old but neatly pressed
                              and clunky black shoes. He wears
                              a sad expression, too, and I wonder
                              if life has been unkind to him,
                              thinking how awful it would be to
                              have a third-rate sitcom as the
                              crowning achievement of your artistic
                              career, to be reduced to taking the
                              subway and having people recognize
                              you (if you're lucky) for the wimp
                              you played, maybe remembering the name
                              of the smirking brat who played your son
                              (Jay North) but never yours or any of
                              the program's other grownups, who by now
                              are dead (Mr. Wilson, R.I.P.) or grayheads
                              like you. I'd look sad too, I think, as
                              he walks out of the car at Penn Station.

Not Stravinsky

Dark-eyed boy in tight designer jeans and sneakers on your way
from basketball practice at Bishop Somebody High, I

don't know what you're playing on your Walkman but it probably is
not Stravinsky.

Summer, South Brooklyn

gusher in the street where bald men with cigars
watch as boys in gym shorts and no shirts
crack the hydrant, rinsing yet another car
a daily ritual, these street-wide spurts

of city water over rich brown and deep white
of ranch wagon and arrogant sedan
whose "opera windows" seem less *arriviste* than trite
they shake the water from their hair, shake hands

with neighbors passing, passing generations
I watch and am not part of, for the block is theirs
by family and tradition, and I'm no relation
an opera drowned by disco beat, draw stares

from big boys with big radios that might outlast them
brace myself for insults I recall
forgetting the adult they see when I stride past them
until I realize they're kids, that's all

New Music

The lovemaking grows more intense, not less.
Ten million men and women out of work
The price of a sound currency. Tim Page
Brings us "The New, The Old, The Unexpected,"
Two hours of new music every day,
Six hours of sleep, eight of work, and art
Simmers on the back burner with desire
For Fame, for Fortune. Rules: choose one, not both.

The reasons for not moving grow more lame.
Ten million stories in this naked city
And one of them is ours. I'm like Tim Miller
Spraying my name in paint upon my chest,
Reminding me of who I am. A man
By any other name's a refugee.
I shall not back away, but take my stand
Where love and honesty are one, not both.

It gets more complicated with the years
And less so. There must be ten million ways
Of making love, but all I need are three:
The new, the old, the unexpected. Grace
Is like New Music hitting with the force
Of tidal waves, or like the atmosphere
So clear these mornings we forget it's how
We've always lived and breathed as one, not both.

I touch you on the eyes, and chest, and wrist.
Ten million dollars wouldn't change a thing,
The price of a sound mind. "Tim Dlugos knows,"
Voice-over from an old-time radio
Reminding me of where I used to be.
I'm here, and so are you. To make it art
Is easy when you're musical as we.
Live it or live with it: choose one, not both.

Psalm

Each year I forget the simple fact
that spring's new leaves are of a sickly
hue, Lord; not at all the strong dark
green in Wallace Nutting silver-prints
of my youth. You remember: the country
lane a dozen miles from Boston running
past a field where the amazing pink
of dogwood and white of apple blossom posed
against high summer verdure, dark and beckoning.
Not so the oak by yonder carriage-house.
Call that green? It's half yellow, and its bark
is gray, not brown — no, silver today.
Clouds behind the clouds behind the yellow
clouds upstage, and behind them all a vast
emptiness, if the naked eye can be
believed. It can't, as You and science teach.
Teenaged children throw a ball around the street,
speed it on its way with expletives, while pre-
schoolers with their stately gait have their
ball, too, this one phosphorescent in a tiny
hand, a place to focus in the changing light,
which doesn't fade, but shifts perspective,
like the slim retarded girl in the gray or silver
make-believe fur who waits each afternoon
on the stoop or corner for the kids who play ball
to walk past and smile. I'm waiting, too.
Like a Doberman longs for an enormous field
big enough to run across as hard and as far
as it can; like Mr. Ahmed longs for a prospective
buyer to walk in so he can unload the Arabia
Felix Restaurant and happily return to the stony
village whose photograph adorns his menu; like
a bourgeois idealist longs to see the world
through Wallace Nutting's eyes, in which

the chlorophyll does its job right; so my soul
longs for You, Lord, for the vast amused amazement
of your grace, in this your Strong (and holy) Place.

To Walter Lowenfels

You had four real ones of your own, so why
did you write *To an Imaginary
Daughter*? I found it in the Books
for a Buck bin at Barnes & Noble,
your signature inside, a copy you'd inscribed
to someone whom you'd just rejected
for one of your anthologies of wooly
Movement writing, to which you gave your life
in language of your time, the Great Depression.
It's depressing how unrecognizable
your name's become; with Hemingway and
Henry Miller, one of the three
most prominent and best expatriate
writers in Paris; author of *Steel*,
the pamphlet that made bosses of the day
see Red. Your popularity
like vaunted winds of change, swept through
the corners of the world lit by Left-Lit
and out the window, like the wind today
that drove me into Barnes & Noble.
It's cold out there when no one knows
your name. Spokesman, working-class
Whitmanic bard, poet of the brave
new world, speaker of demotic
democratic truths, mover and shaker, shock-troop
of the Revolution, too-accessible
parent of forgotten books: I know your slim
affected and affecting offspring
only because some miffed, less-than-forgotten
scribbler sold it off for change.
The verdict of the History you used
as engine and excuse is not in yet,
you'd say. I'll stick around.
But I'm haunted by the lack of rhyme

and reason in how power dwindles down
from clarity and massive sweep
of language to a garrulous old man
in Peekskill serving French bread and Bordeaux
to luncheon guests. "He wore a black beret;
the old days were important to him."

Father of vanished texts, where went your truth?
The wind has cleared away your agitprop,
your art, your bromides, your imaginings
of world, or word, or children strong of grip
enough to clasp, to spare your voice.

Dear heart, wish you or I were here or there . . .
No. That's not true.
I wish I knew that you
were happy now, and sure at last
of being loved. I loved
our long talks late at night
when all the others were in bed. We'd fight
about the war and Watergate, and sip
Virginia Gentleman (one was your limit).
Your image doesn't dim; it
resonates through all my life.
So many times I've wanted
to call you up or walk downstairs
to your domain, the basement
with its toolbench and pine-paneled
walls, you in a dark mood slouching
over your ham radio, to coax you
back into the light, make you laugh.
Above my desk I have the photograph
of you kneeling beside me in the garden
that the wood absorbed. I'm two and nervous
in the little plastic pool. You're
having a good time with your Number One Son,
smiling more broadly than I can recall
outside of snapshots, though I can remember all
your other faces: stolid in the pew
at church, sublime intentness of a natural
engineer at your electric saw, or soldering
a new attachment to the jerrybuilt
shortwave, red with fury
over being baited or some imaginary
provocation, but mostly
when someone didn't listen.
I see your face the times I wasn't there,
as well: weeping to me on the phone
about the total failure of your life

for a good two hours (I couldn't
decide if you were going bonkers or having
a Pascal-like moment of clear light),
or how you looked the night
of your attack, feeling it come
over you as Ted Koppel asked pithy questions
on the little screen, unable to call out
in answer or for help. I've learned
the difference between a silence
and an absence since your quick
departure. There's no "where"
there, wherever you are. When I talk
to you these days, I end up trying
to convince myself that I'm pretending,
and failing to. It makes me think of you
tapping out a signal like a blind man
on your Morse code key, to strangers
who could understand the special
language that you used, projecting it
along a wire from underground
into the air, into the world.

The Morning

The vitamin-charged slush of Total cereal,
momentum of an early start,
the Breviary's poetry, a flash
of insight from the TV preacher who's dressed
in ever more appalling polyester suits . . .
I shun them. It's the morning,
all I care to know for its duration.
Dream of, of, of . . . can't recall, but
the night before I dreamt I was in bed with someone
I was gaga about. Woke up and there he was,
gaga in his sleep, moans, thrashing.
My nervous clients think I need a thrashing
— "On the stick, you!" — and they're right
on one level, theirs. A story up, I see
an old woman whose arms seem filled with slush
shouting from her window, like Molly Goldberg
on Fifties TV, and I wonder the same thing
I wondered as a tot about the home tube stars:
I see them through a glass, can they see me?
Appropriately darkly. Through the speakers
I learn what Pierre Boulez was getting at
in *Le Marteau sans Maitre*. Un question, Monsieur:
did your hammer demand emancipation
or had it always been a freelance tool?
I risk playing the fool
because this is a world I am creating,
not "text" or "slice of life," and old contexts
don't hold. "Water, water!" A parched prospector
crawls downhill toward the container port.
He plops into the harbor like a grizzled seal,
treads water and surveys the scene.
Stage left: bridges, helicopters overhead.
Stage right: the islands Puerto Rican couples
with tots and prams survey from Bay Ridge Park.

This world's finest anchorage is filled with freighters
which themselves are filled with freight
from everywhere. Drop it here. Then
back through the Narrows to the endless sea.

Pretty Convincing

Talking to my friend Emily, whose drinking
patterns and extravagance of personal
feeling are a lot like mine, I'm pretty
convinced when she explains the things we do
while drinking (a cocktail to celebrate the new
account turns into a party that lasts till 3
a.m. and a terrific hangover) indicate
a problem of a sort I'd not considered.
I've been worried about how I metabolize
the sauce for four years, since my second bout
of hepatitis, when I kissed all the girls
at Christmas dinner and turned bright yellow
Christmas night, but never about whether
I could handle it. It's been more of a given,
the stage set for my life as an artistic queer,
as much of a tradition in these New York circles
as incense for Catholics or German
shepherds for the blind. We re-enact
the rituals, and our faces, like smoky icons
in a certain light, seem to learn nothing
but understand all. It comforts me
yet isn't all that pleasant, like drinking
Ripple to remember high school. A friend
of mine has been drinking in the same bar for decades,
talking to the same types, but progressively
fewer blonds. Joe LeSueur says he's glad
to have been a young man in the Fifties with his
Tab Hunter good looks, because that was the image
men desired; now it's the Puerto Rican
angel with great eyes and a fierce fidelity
that springs out of machismo, rather than a moral
choice. His argument is pretty convincing, too,
except lots of the pretty blonds I've known
default by dying young, leaving the field

to the swarthy. Cameron Burke, the dancer
and waiter at Magoo's, killed on his way home from
the Pines when a car hit his bike on the Sunrise Highway.
Henry Post dead of AIDS, a man I thought would be around
forever, surprising me by his mortality the way
I was surprised when I heard he was not
the grandson of Emily Post at all, just pretending,
like the friend he wrote about in *Playgirl*, Blair Meehan,
was faking when he crashed every A List party for a year
by pretending to be Kay Meehan's son, a masquerade
that ended when a hostess told him "Your mother's here"
and led him by the hand to the dowager — Woman, behold
thy son — underneath a darkening conviction that all,
if not wrong, was not right. By now Henry may have faced
the same embarrassment at some cocktail party in the sky.
Stay as outrageously nasty as you were. And Patrick
Mack, locked into my memory as he held court in the Anvil
by the downstairs pinball machine, and writhing
as he danced in Lita Hornick's parlor when the Stimulators
played her party, dead last week of causes I don't know,
as if the cause and not the effect were the problem.
My blond friend Chuck Shaw refers to the Bone-
crusher in the Sky, and I'm starting to
imagine a road to his castle lit by radiant
heads of blonds on poles as streetlamps for the gods,
flickering on at twilight as I used to do
in the years when I crashed more parties and acted
more outrageously and met more beauties and made
more enemies than ever before or ever again, I pray.
It's spring and there's another crop of kids
with haircuts from my childhood and inflated self-esteem
from my arrival in New York, who plug into the history
of prettiness, convincing to themselves and the devout.
We who are about to catch the eye of someone
new salute as the cotillion passes, led by blonds
and followed by the rest of us, a formal march
to the dark edge of the ballroom where we step out

onto the terrace and the buds on the forsythia
that hides the trash sprout magically
at our approach. I toast it
as memorial to dreams as fragile and persistent
as a blond in love. My clothes smell like the smoky
bar, but the sweetness of the April air's
delicious when I step outside and fill
my lungs, leaning my head back
in a first-class seat on the shuttle
between the rowdy celebration of great deeds
to come and an enormous Irish wake in which
the corpses change but the party goes on forever.

Spinner

If Plato's right, my "you" is a reflection
of years-ago phenomena, the way I felt
when faced with your unquenchable erection
and well of nervous energy, that let you belt

the latest songs and dance till sunrise,
high as a kite whose string I held. You were as sweet
as your nightly two desserts, as unwise
as I, and just as loath to meet

unpleasantness head-on, as when you told me
that we were through. "Impossible," I said,
a disbelief that still enfolds me
when I wake and remember that you're dead.

I'm writing to your shadow, which recedes
with youth we shared and spent, to fill
the absence of your voice, my dull need.
Ghost of a ghost, this puts you farther still.

The Fruit Streets

There's a little cottage in the back
of a composed facade. I want
to live there. There's a little
composition I can doodle on the keys
in basic chords. The man with an electric
speaker where his voice should be
in corduroy is sweeping down
the Fruit Streets, as a lady
inside my cloudy memory of other lives
or movies sweeps the cobblestones
with her train. She's on her way
to Pilgrim Church, where Beecher thunders.
Rain sweeps in from the bay.
I wonder how much good a sermon
can do, though they were once as popular
as cautionary soaps about the rich
to rubes today. Within the stiffness
of a form and collar let me touch
your eyes, take your hand. I'll lead you
to a land of colors — Cranberry, Pineapple,
Orange and the spurious Joralemon — and thrilling
tastes. The rawness of the wind is softened
by a blast of citrus, as the view
from the Heights gains pigment with a flick
of the Tint dial. It's a new world
out there, as if a box of Trix
had spilled across the harbor where the grays
and silvers played beneath a sky they perfectly
resembled. In the glow of an ass-backwards
native lore, Paradise could be as sudden
as a bite of fruit, or death
to the congregants. Protestants
find both "forbidden," though the preacher
whose words moved a government himself

may have brewed the metaphor while doodling
with a colleague's wife. The life
of the flesh is lived inside a sack
of flesh, but the life of the memory
is spun out in the names by which
we know the streets. It was here
I smoked a joint with John before he left
to turn into a rock star on the Coast
and watched the fireworks.
They lit up the sky,
Cranberry red, Pineapple yellow,
Orange orange, against the electric
blue-engorged horizon, radiant scrim
you can point to any twilight on your way
to drinks with friends, silly rabbits.
Pellets of our histories have piled up
in my mind, the Nation's Attic,
a nation carried onward by the names
of streets and Protestants like Carrie Nation,
where hatchets that remain unburied
reduce saloons to slivers. There's a beam
of pale light playing on a chink between
the landmark's bricks, a sliver of decay.
It's colorless, a paradigm of how I want to look
to let you see through what I say to find
the cottage with the patch of lawn where I live,
a dooryard in the patchwork of a city
you know about because you've heard it
in my voice, as if by faith.

Healing the World From Battery Park

Om Tara
Tu Tara
Ture Svaha
      TIBETAN MANTRA

Draw a deep breath. Hold it. Let it go.
That's the smell of the ocean.
Our forebears hailed from out there. There's a stele
to mark the spot where Minuit exchanged
a mess of beads and trinkets for this island.
He may have thought it proof he was
a clever trader, although if the sky
were sky-blue as today, the sunlight's flash
through bright glass would have been magnificent,
and that might have had tremendous value
in another culture. In another language,
"minuit" 's a division of the day.
I've divided my days among a host
of places near the sea. I get a lot
of comfort when I walk a beach, or through
the narrow streets among a crush of traders.
Sand in my shoes, sand of the Castle
Clinton courtyard where all of New York
turned out of yore to see the Jacksons,
Andrew and his wife. He'd whipped the bloody
British in the town of New Orleans
and massacred the Creeks. His steely eyes,
as blue as western skies, saw the space I see.
He breathed the same air. There's a little part
of him in me, that wants to drive away
the savages who populate the dark
expanse beyond the porch light's reach.
It takes a Trail of Tears to teach
that neighborhood improvement's not the point.

May the breath I draw become a balm
to soothe the exiled people of all times
and lands: the Cherokee, the Jew,
the people of Tibet whose loss brought us
abundant wisdom, the kulak and the Sioux,
the lover I abandoned and the friends
I drove away, the difficult and friendless
kicked out by their family, their school,
their church, their boss, their spouse, who found them too
impossible to put up with for one more minute.
In this park, their refuge, I divide my time
and feed it to the world when I exhale
like bread for ducks. It's not a fantasy
of power, and it's not about the rediscovery
of arcane treasure from a better place,
quieter and more romantic, like Tara
in the days of kings or in the antebellum
South. It's about the light that permeates
the sky above the boathouse where the sloop-
for-hire is moored. One romantic night,
it sailed across the harbor with my love
and me aboard. We drank champagne, and trailed
our fingers through the surface of the oil-
and-water stew that buoyed us. When we grew
apart, the two halves of a single wake
that break on banks across the dark expanse
of river from each other, I chose rage
to hold my sorrow's head beneath the waves
until I couldn't feel it anymore,
though somewhere under driftwood-littered slips
or in the trash-strewn slime a fathom down,
I knew that it was hiding. May the breath
I draw become a healing touch
to ease the pain I caused him, and to speed
the light that passed between and through us on
to its next stop. Here I divide my heart
among the teenaged couples and the shy

or clandestine romantics from the big
law firms who nuzzle on a bench, and queens
in stained Quiana shirts who cruise between
the slabs of stone with names of boys who died
in World War II. May it soothe my father,
who couldn't say how very much he loved
his wife, and all the tongue-tied men. And may
it heal the women, too; millions
like my mother who are left behind
when what they love about a man is wrenched
out of his body, hidden in another place.
In another language, "Tara" is the name
of a she-god sprung out of a human tear.
She heals all wounds and brings the world a sense
of peace. On this island where the gods
would outnumber the humans in a week if such
a mode of birth became habitual,
I beg her presence as I feel my breath
flying like a jet from Newark
out into the world. There's a quantity
of tenderness I feel sometimes
that drops into my chest precipitous
and golden as the sun into Fort Lee.
I couldn't tell you where it comes from, but
I'm learning where it hides. It's in the nectarine
you ate for breakfast, or the thing
you're doing now, not in what you think
you should do or in what comes next.
And it's not in what you think "God" means;
the only certainty is that you're wrong.
Draw a deep breath. Thank you, mother.
Hold the light inside and let it find
the ragged spots, a gentle tongue to probe
for caries. Then expire.
A little part of you is in the wind now,
a trace of pain or coffee in the scent
of brine that clasps you like a lover,

closer and more faithful than a lover.
Bless me, father. This is my first
confession: I'm living in the light
at the bottom of a sea of air,
everything I need in a place I share
with everyone. It's in your hands.

July
for Darragh Park

The foot should never go where the eye has already been.
                                                CAPABILITY BROWN

I knew the place had capabilities
the moment that I saw it. How the house
stands sideways, for one thing; the front porch view
is of the lowland garden and the swamp,
not Mecox Road. I had them bring a crane
two years ago and excavate a pond.
There's no place you can stand and see the whole
of it, a trick that Brown used when he built
the lake at Stowe. The prospect from the knoll
where the house sits is very much like Stowe
sans folly and tempietto, though the plants
are all indigenous. Along the path
that winds down to the swamp, I've placed the reds:
bayberry in clumps, and trumpet-vines
on higher ground. I planted the tall reeds
myself, in hipboots, clearing out a years-
old jungle which is growing back so fast
I'll have to stock with Chinese grass carp, which
can grow to twenty pounds, a sort of Sumo
minnow that feeds on waterweeds. I hope
they don't eat lilypads. On the steep slope
beyond the pond's a sea of chicory;
it all goes blue next month. I've put some blue
lobelia there, too; off-blue, towards red.
The sequence of their blooming makes the view
change every week all summer. Light. Dark. Light.
It keeps the eye engaged with every step,
whether you want some inspiration or
a tussy-mussy (it's a word of Vita
Sackville-West's, means "wildflower bouquet."
I spent some hours making one today).

The path you can't see, over by the shed,
is verged by ailanthus; in a year
or three, the branches will have overgrown
to form a shady tunnel. At its end
I'll place another garden, which will block
the sight of houses going up like weeds
from here to Job's Lane Beach. At the high point
of their influence, Brown and Repton moved
whole villages whose jumble interfered
with one long view. *That's* capability.
Behind the ailanthus, in the woods,
I'll put in a spring garden by-and-by,
lady's slipper and jack-in-the-pulpit.
When you're heading down the hill or through
the meadow, there's no way you can tell, but
all the paths are spokes which lead you back
to one place, the lawn with the butternut
as hub, a spreading Tree of Life, as in
the *Roman de la Rose* or Genesis.
I wanted something right there for the eye
to focus on. Then I remembered Fairfield
Porter's painting called "July," with those
white Adirondack chairs. They're perfect there.
See how the white turns pale blue as the night
creeps in, full of mosquitoes and fireflies.
And don't be frightened by the strangled cries
from the swamp; those are peepers bellowing,
not *Psycho III*. The sounds and smells grow dense
this time of evening. The mock-tympanum
lugubriously beaten by the waves
a mile away sounds muffled in its quilt
of fog. The cooling air is redolent
of linden by the porch; its flowerets
will burst next week. I'll celebrate with friends,
throw a festival. The lurcher comes inside
and dampness clambers uphill from the pond
or blows in from the beachfront. There's a spot

of cloud against the night sky. Dark. Light. Dark.
It blossoms downward, filling up the yard.
Pretty soon your hand before your face
will be the farthest prospect you can see,
delight in. It's familiar by now,
the rote procession into night, and oddly
comforting, like music I recall:
a blues lament that all the things you loved
have disappeared, and you might as well be
anywhere, underlaid by gentle drums
that let you know you're near the ocean.

Here Comes the Bride

Ironweed, beggarweed, joe pye weed,
the Huck-Finn-threading-his-raft-among-the-stiffs-
and-driftwood feeling that a fellow gets
slapping with his paddle at the silt
and the gaseous muck he slogs through on the trek
to land. Then a cloud moves.
All those purple flowers that the streak
of purple on the endless-shades-of-green
shore signified from a midafternoon
midriver point of view become a hundred
sheaves of light. I learned their names from a book
that someone gave me in another world,
the one I came from, where adrenalin
runs like a river through the jittery day.
I've come out of the current like a girl
who thinks it's time to change
her name to something simpler, and is looking
for a way. They say folks out here work
while the light lasts, the light that outlasts them.
It's hard to tell what time it is this time
of day; these parts don't change until the sun
breaks through and bathes the river in the gentlest
glow I know. I've been there.
I'm wedded to the notion of a living
and a life awash in it, a series of tableaus
as self-contained as frames of film
where change comes imperceptibly. "That field
was carpeted in purple just a week ago;
now it's all gone to seed." When I was single,
I had the most insane adventures.
Now that I'm married, I've nothing
but the path in front of me, the wide one
to the house with the big front porch
whose light will go on in a little while.

1988–1990

Retrovir

Turn
back oh man
and see how where you've come from
looks from here: the light-
filled leak of sunrise, drone
of morning's clarity and fleeting sense
of firm direction, lunch with wine,
siesta and the afternoon you're part of.
Here the sky is always blue
and white, the colors of the pills
that poison you while they extend your life,
inoculating you with time
that draws you back with fingers
curved around the bowstring.
You are not the target, you're the arrow

73

and the dirty wind that hits
your face on summer streets these
too-long evenings means you're moving
faster than you know, a shrill
projectile through the neutral air
above a world war, headed for the flesh
of someone's notion of croquet
at twilight on the lawn. The thickening
damp crowds out the light, as green
of grass and fountain separates
to blue and white.

Ordinary Time

Which are the magic
moments in ordinary
time? All of them,
for those who can see.
That is what redemption
means, I decide
at the meeting. Then
walk with David wearing
his new Yale T-shirt
and new long hair to 103.
Leonard and Eileen come, too.
Leonard wears a shark's tooth
on a chain around his neck
and long blond hair.
These days he's the manager
of Boots and Saddles ("Bras
and Girdles," my beloved
Bobby used to say) and
costumer for the Gay Cable
Network's *Dating Game*.
One week the announcer is
a rhinestone cowboy, sequin
shirt and black fur chaps,
the next a leatherman, etc.
Eileen's crewcut makes
her face light up.
Underneath our hairstyles,
23 years of sobriety, all told —
the age of a girl who's "not
so young but not so very old,"
wrote Berryman, who flew
from his recovery with the force
of a poet hitting bottom.
It's not the way I choose

to go out of this restaurant
or day today, and I
have a choice. Wanda
the comedian comes over
to our table. "Call me
wicked Wanda," she smirks
when we're introduced.
Why is New York City
awash in stand-up comics
at the least funny point
in its history? Still,
some things stay the same.
People wonder what the people
in their buildings would think
if the ones who are wondering
became incredibly famous,
as famous as Madonna.
Debby Harry lived in Eileen's
building in the Village
in the early seventies, and she
was just the shy girl
in the band upstairs.
Poets read the writing
of their friends, and
are happy when they like it
thoroughly, when the work's
that good and the crippling
sense of competition stays away.
Trips get planned: David
home to California, Eileen
to New Mexico, Chris and I
to France and Spain, on vectors
which will spread out
from a single point, like ribs
of an umbrella. Then
after the comfort of a wedge
of blueberry peach pie and cup

of Decaf, sober friends
thread separate ways home
through the maze of blankets
on the sidewalk covered with
the scraps of someone else's life.
Mine consists of understanding
that the magic isn't something
that I make, but something
that shines through the things
I make and do and say
the way a brooch or scrap of fabric
shines from the detritus
to catch Leonard's eye
and be of use for costumes,
when I am fearless and thorough
enough to give it room,
all the room there is in ordinary
time, which embraces all
the people and events and hopes
that choke the street tonight
and still leaves room for everyone
and everything and every
other place, the undescribed
and indescribable, more various
and cacaphonous than voice
can tell or mind conceive,
and for the sky's vast depths
from which they're all
a speck of light.

Signs of Madness

Recognizing strings
of coincidence as having
baleful or hermetic meaning,
e.g. the fact that each
of Ronald Wilson
Reagan's three names has
six letters, Mark of
the Apocalyptic Beast,
languorous and toothless
though it would have to be
to fit that application.
Smelling burning flesh
or sulphur, or a sweet
antibiotic sweat that
leaches into sheets
and pillows, like the smell
my mother had when she was
dying, or the one I suddenly
developed in the weeks before
I came down with AIDS.
Muttering at motorists
in other cars, hearing
one's own voice pronounce
unspoken imprecation.
Wanting to impose Islamic
law for lapses of behavior
or taste within the city limits.
Limiting one's television
fare to programs one recalls
from childhood. Wanting
to call childhood friends
and ask them how they're doing,
how their lives have changed
since junior high. Memorizing

names of senators, bishops
of the church, or nominees for
Vice President from major
parties, and reciting them
at night to get to sleep.
Listing signs that all
may be no more right
in one's mind than is right
in the world, and feeling
less anxiety from identifying
symptoms in one's thinking and
behavior than comfort
in the list's existence
and delight at having
called it forth.

All Souls' Day

Faithful depart in swarms, like holiday
Or weekend mobs that throng the underground
Republic of commuters, on their way
Against the odds to someplace nicer. Round
My hospital bed, rosebuds, and beyond
Yellow hibiscus on the windowsill,
Gauze crisscrosses blue sky. Is it a fond
Evasion to imagine that we will
Relax into a gently-lit eclipse
So porous and expansive it derails
Time like a train, absorbing dark details
Life's action-painter imitation drips
Each second on each soul that aches to be
Revived, restored, on all souls? Probably.

Parable
(after Mark 4: 11–12)

Within the yarn, a needle
has been hidden. That's
the point, whatever message
one can find behind the words.
That dishwater contains
shards of a crystal tumbler
might be more important
than submerged utensils' function
at meals or as metaphor,
at least to the humming hausfrau,
one of the domestic types
who populate this sort of narrative.
She's wearing yellow Living Gloves
that reach up to her elbows.
Their deep cuffs are a pleasure.
It's a good clean feeling
to plunge one's hands
into those great white suds,
but what one grasps may be
no fruit plate, but the sharp
and sinking insight that within
the homeliest arrangements
lurks a secret that can change
one's life or cause
real pain. You see
the cut and hear the scream,
but don't perceive or understand
and aren't supposed to,
lest you be forgiven.

Powerless

I was a mess. I felt like crying
all the time. No matter what
I said, how charming I would try
to be, my friends, old friends
I thought I could depend on,
looked at me like I was crazy
or depraved. They were the ones
I'd called for years on mornings
after blackouts I perceived
as rip-roaring adventures.
"What happened? Was I too
outrageous?" These days
the answer was obviously yes, but
I was powerless to stop. I didn't know
the drinking was the cause; I thought
it was the upshot of the sad
departure of my looks and mind and hope
and friends and gifts and sense
that anything could ever feel other
than stripped of joy and dropped
into the sea in concrete overshoes again.
I was dying, lying
in a bed I couldn't even lure
a hustler into, in a rock-and-roll
motel on Santa Monica
where Madness partied all night
by the pool, and Tom Waits
used to live, a place I thought was cool
to say I stayed at, though I didn't
feel so hot when I awoke
to light that made me want
to vomit, reaching for the Bud
I'd passed out next to, thinking
that if I could choke down last night's

beer it was a form of completion
at a time when I could never finish
anything, and couldn't even
step back from the panic anymore
with a drink to make me think
my pain was my participation
in the life of poetry I'd chosen.
I wanted to be stoic at the lot
I'd drawn by being such an artist.
I wanted to be captain of my soul,
but I was out of control at the helm
of a scow I'd steered into the rocks,
horrified to watch its cargo
of self-involved self-pity
poison the environment I loved.
I couldn't stop the dark
from spreading, couldn't plug the leaks,
couldn't scrub the filth away, and
it was all my fault.
Then something odd happened.
I woke up in my motel room
in the middle of the night.
No one else was there,
but I had the strongest sense
that somebody was with me,
sitting on the bed, in fact.
It was as if my hand were being
held. I thought of that old film
The Haunting, where something
similar happens to Julie Harris.
But this wasn't scary. I lay there
and felt myself surrounded by the presence
of the gentlest, most compassionate
and loving — person? I'm not sure —
that I had ever known. There was
no hand that I could see, but
I clung to it. There was no voice

as such, and yet I clearly heard the words,
"Everything will be all right." I wondered
if this could be a visit from the Virgin Mary,
the kind I always wanted as a kid.
I was surprised how calm
and undramatic it all was.
I let the love wash over me
until I fell asleep again.
The next day was Mother's Day.
I made a call and went to my first
meeting a few blocks away. I'd been wondering
where all the healthy, handsome people
in West Hollywood had disappeared to.
I found out. An old guy
with a shaven head and twenty years
spoke first. He said, "I say
two prayers each morning. The first
is 'Thank you.' The second is
'Don't let me fuck this up.'"
I say those prayers today.
These things took place five years ago.
I didn't dream them up
or make them happen.
I was powerless to change
the horror and the shame
that had infected my whole life.
I know that they were lifted
by the power of whatever
held my hand that night.
This is not about religion,
not about belief. I know what happened.
I was there; *it* was there.
Nothing can change that.

G-9

I'm at a double wake
in Springfield, for a childhood
friend and his father
who died years ago. I join
my aunt in the queue of mourners
and walk into a brown study,
a sepia room with books
and magazines. The father's
in a coffin; he looks exhumed,
the worse for wear. But where
my friend's remains should be
there's just the empty base
of an urn. Where are his ashes?
His mother hands me
a paper cup with pills:
leucovorin, Zovirax,
and AZT. "Henry
wanted you to have these,"
she sneers. "Take all
you want, for all the good
they'll do." "Dlugos.
Meester Dlugos." A lamp
snaps on. Raquel,
not Welch, the chubby
nurse, is standing by my bed.
It's 6 a.m., time to flush
the heplock and hook up
the I.V. line. False dawn
is changing into day, infusing
the sky above the Hudson
with a flush of light.
My roommate stirs
beyond the pinstriped curtain.
My first time here on G-9,

the AIDS ward, the cheery
D & D Building intentionality
of the decor made me feel
like jumping out a window.
I'd been lying on a gurney
in an E.R. corridor
for nineteen hours, next to
a psychotic druggie
with a voice like Abbie
Hoffman's. He was tied
up, or down, with strips
of cloth (he'd tried to slug
a nurse) and sent up
a grating adenoidal whine
all night. "Nurse ... nurse ...
untie me, *please* ... these
rags have strange powers."
By the time they found
a bed for me, I was in
no mood to appreciate the clever
curtains in my room,
the same fabric exactly
as the drapes and sheets
of a P-town guest house
in which I once — partied? stayed?
All I can remember is
the pattern. Nor did it
help to have the biggest queen
on the nursing staff
clap his hands delightedly
and welcome me to AIDS-land.
I wanted to drop
dead immediately. That
was the low point. Today
these people are my friends,
in the process of restoring
me to life a second time.

I can walk and talk
and breathe simultaneously
now. I draw a breath
and sing "Happy Birthday"
to my roommate Joe.
He's 51 today. I didn't think
he'd make it. Three weeks
ago they told him that he had
aplastic anemia, and nothing
could be done. Joe had been
a rotten patient, moaning
operatically, throwing chairs
at nurses. When he got
the bad news, there was
a big change. He called
the relatives with whom
he had been disaffected,

was anointed and communicated
for the first time since the age
of eight when he was raped
by a priest, and made a will.
As death drew nearer, Joe
grew nicer, almost serene.
Then the anemia
began to disappear, not
because of medicines, but
on its own. Ready to die,
it looks like Joe has more
of life to go. He'll go
home soon. "When will *you*
get out of here?" he asks me.
I don't know; when the X-ray
shows no more pneumonia.
I've been here three weeks
this time. What have I
accomplished? Read some
Balzac, spent "quality

time" with friends, come back
from death's door, and
prayed, prayed a lot.
Barry Bragg, a former
lover of a former
lover and a new
Episcopalian, has AIDS too,
and gave me a leatherbound
and gold-trimmed copy of the Office,
the one with all the antiphons.
My list of daily intercessions
is as long as a Russian
novel. I pray about AIDS
last. Last week I made a list
of all my friends who've died
or who are living and infected.
Every day since, I've remembered
someone I forgot to list.
This morning it was Chasen
Gaver, the performance poet
from DC. I don't know
if he's still around. I liked
him and could never stand
his poetry, which made it
difficult to be a friend,
although I wanted to defend
him one excruciating night
at a Folio reading, where
Chasen snapped his fingers
and danced around spouting
frothy nonsense about Andy
Warhol to the rolling eyes
of self-important "language-
centered" poets, whose dismissive
attitude and ugly manners
were worse by far than anything
that Chasen ever wrote.

Charles was his real name;
a classmate at Antioch
dubbed him "Chasen," after
the restaurant, I guess.
Once I start remembering,
so much comes back.
There are forty-nine names
on my list of the dead,
thirty-two names of the sick.
Cookie Mueller changed
lists Saturday. They all
will, I guess, the living,
I mean, unless I go
before them, in which case
I may be on somebody's
list myself. It's hard
to imagine so many people
I love dying, but no harder
than to comprehend so many
already gone. My beloved
Bobby, maniac and boyfriend.
Barry reminded me that he
had sex with Bobby
on the coat pile at his Christmas
party, two years in a row.
That's the way our life
together used to be, a lot
of great adventures. Who'll
remember Bobby's stories
about driving in his debutante
date's father's white Mercedes
from hole to hole of the golf course
at the poshest country club
in Birmingham at 3 a.m.,
or taking off his clothes
in the redneck bar on a dare,
or working on *Stay Hungry*

as the dresser of a then-
unknown named Schwarzenegger.
Who will be around to anthologize
his purple cracker similes:
"Sweatin' like a nigger
on Election Day," "Hotter
than a half-fucked fox
in a forest fire." The ones
that I remember have to do
with heat, Bobby shirtless,
sweating on the dance floor
of the tiny bar in what is now
a shelter for the indigent
with AIDS on the dockstrip,
stripping shirts off Chuck Shaw,
Barry Bragg and me, rolling
up the torn rags, using them
as pom-poms, then bolting
off down West Street, gracefully
(despite the overwhelming
weight of his inebriation)
vaulting over trash cans
as he sang, "I like to be
in America" in a Puerto Rican
accent. When I pass,
who'll remember, who will care
about these joys and wonders?
I'm haunted by that more
than by the faces
of the dead and dying.
A speaker crackles near
my bed and nurses
streak down the corridor.
The black guy on the respirator
next door bought the farm,
Maria tells me later, but
only when I ask. She has tears

in her eyes. She'd known him
since his first day on G-9
a long time ago. Will I also
become a fond, fondly regarded
regular, back for stays
the way retired retiring
widowers return to the hotel
in Nova Scotia or Provence
where they vacationed with
their wives? I expect so, although
that's down the road; today's
enough to fill my plate. A bell
rings, like the gong that marks
the start of a fight. It's 10
and Derek's here to make
the bed, Derek who at 16
saw Bob Marley's funeral
in the football stadium
in Kingston, hot tears
pouring down his face.
He sings as he folds
linens, "You can fool
some of the people some
of the time," dancing
a little softshoe as he works.
There's a reason he came in
just now; *Divorce Court*
drones on Joe's TV, and
Derek is hooked. I can't
believe the script is plausible
to him, Jamaican hipster
that he is, but he stands
transfixed by the parade
of faithless wives and screwed-up
husbands. The judge is testy;
so am I, unwilling
auditor of drivel. Phone

my friends to block it out:
David, Jane and Eileen. I missed
the bash for David's magazine
on Monday and Eileen's reading
last night. Jane says that
Marie-Christine flew off
to Marseilles where her mother
has cancer of the brain,
reminding me that AIDS
is just a tiny fragment
of life's pain. Eileen has
been thinking about Bobby, too,
the dinner that we threw
when he returned to New York
after getting sick. Pencil-thin,
disfigured by KS, he held forth
with as much kinetic charm
as ever. What we have
to cherish is not only
what we can recall of how
things were before the plague,
but how we each responded
once it started. People
have been great to me.
An avalanche of love
has come my way
since I got sick, and not
just moral support.
Jaime's on the board
of PEN's new fund
for AIDS; he's helping out.
Don Windham slipped a check
inside a note, and Brad
Gooch got me something
from the Howard Brookner Fund.
Who'd have thought when we
dressed up in ladies'

clothes for a night for a hoot
in Brad ("June Buntt") and
Howard ("Lili La Lean")'s suite
at the Chelsea that things
would have turned out this way:
Howard dead at 35, Chris Cox
("Kay Sera Sera")'s friend Bill
gone too, "Bernadette of Lourdes"
(guess who) with AIDS,
God knows how many positive.
Those 14th Street wigs and enormous
stingers and Martinis don't
provoke nostalgia for a time
when love and death were less
inextricably linked, but
for the stories we would tell
the morning after, best

when they involved our friends,
second-best, our heroes.
J.J. Mitchell was a master
of the genre. When he learned
he had AIDS, I told him
he should write them down.
His mind went first. I'll tell you
one of his best. J.J. was
Jerome Robbins' houseguest
at Bridgehampton. Every morning
they would have a contest
to see who could finish
the *Times* crossword first.
Robbins always won, until
a day when he was clearly
baffled. Grumbling, scratching
over letters, he finally
threw his pen down. "J.J.,
tell me what I'm doing wrong."
One clue was "Great 20th-c.

choreographer." The solution
was "Massine," but Robbins
had placed his own name
in the space. Every word
around it had been changed
to try to make the puzzle
work, except that answer.
At this point there'd be
a horsey laugh from J.J.
— "Isn't that *great*?"
he'd say through clenched
teeth ("Locust Valley lockjaw").
It was, and there were lots
more where that one came from,
only you can't get there anymore.
He's dropped into the maw
waiting for the G-9
denizens and for all flesh,
as silent as the hearts
that beat upon the beds
up here: the heart of the drop-
dead beautiful East Village
kid who came in yesterday,
Charles Frost's heart nine inches
from the spleen they're taking
out tomorrow, the heart of
the demented girl whose screams
roll down the hallways
late at night, hearts that long
for lovers, for reprieve,
for old lives, for another chance.
My heart, so calm most days,
sinks like a brick
to think of all that heartache.
I've been staying sane with
program tools, turning everything
over to God "as I understand

him." I don't understand him.
Thank God I read so much
Calvin last spring; the absolute
necessity of blind obedience
to a sometimes comforting,
sometimes repellent, always
incomprehensible Source
of light and life stayed
with me. God can seem
so foreign, a parent
from another country,
like my Dad and his own
father speaking Polish
in the kitchen. I wouldn't
trust a father or a God
too much like me, though.
That is why I pack up all
my cares and woes, and load them
on the conveyor belt, the speed
of which I can't control, like
Chaplin on the assembly line
in *Modern Times* or Lucy on TV.
I don't need to run
machines today. I'm standing
on a moving sidewalk
headed for the dark
or light, whatever's there.
Duncan Hannah visits, and
we talk of out-of-body
experiences. His was
amazing. Bingeing on vodka
in his dorm at Bard, he woke
to see a naked boy
in fetal posture on the floor.
Was it a corpse, a classmate,
a pickup from the blackout
of the previous night? Duncan

didn't know. He struggled
out of bed, walked over
to the youth, and touched
his shoulder. The boy turned;
it was Duncan himself.
My own experience was
milder, don't make me flee
screaming from the room
as Duncan did. It happened
on a Tibetan meditation
weekend at the Cowley Fathers'
house in Cambridge.
Michael Koonsman led it,
healer whose enormous paws
directed energy. He touched
my spine to straighten up
my posture, and I gasped
at the rush. We were chanting

to Tara, goddess of compassion
and peace, in the basement chapel
late at night. I felt myself
drawn upward, not levitating
physically, but still somehow
above my body. A sense
of bliss surrounded me.
It lasted ten or fifteen
minutes. When I came down,
my forehead hurt. The spot
where the "third eye" appears
in Buddhist art felt
as though someone had pushed
a pencil through it.
The soreness lasted for a week.
Michael wasn't surprised.
He did a lot of work
with people with AIDS
in the epidemic's early days,

but when he started losing
weight and having trouble
with a cough, he was filled
with denial. By the time
he checked into St. Luke's,
he was in dreadful shape.
The respirator down his throat
squelched the contagious
enthusiasm of his voice,
but he could still spell out
what he wanted to say
on a plastic Ouija board
beside his bed. When
the doctor who came in
to tell him the results
of his bronchoscopy said,
"Father, I'm afraid I have
bad news," Michael grabbed
the board and spelled,
"The truth is always
Good News." After he died,
I had a dream in which
I was a student in a class
that he was posthumously
teaching. With mock annoyance
he exclaimed, "Oh, Tim!
I can't believe you really think
that AIDS is a disease!"
There's evidence in that
direction, I'll tell him
if the dream recurs: the shiny
hamburger-in-lucite look
of the big lesion on my face;
the smaller ones I daub
with makeup; the loss
of forty pounds in a year;
the fatigue that comes on

at the least convenient times.
The symptoms float like algae
on the surface of the grace
that buoys me up today.
Arthur comes in with
the Sacrament, and we have
to leave the room (Joe's
Italian family has arrived
for birthday cheer) to find
some quiet. Walk out
to the breezeway, where
it might as well be
August for the stifling
heat. On Amsterdam,
pedestrians and drivers are
oblivious to our small aerie,
as we peer through the grille
like cloistered nuns. Since
leaving G-9 the first time,
I always slow my car down
on this block, and stare up
at this window, to the unit
where my life was saved.
It's strange how quickly
hospitals feel foreign
when you leave, and how normal
their conventions seem as soon
as you check in. From below,
it's like checking out the windows
of the West Street Jail; hard
to imagine what goes on there,
even if you know firsthand.
The sun is going down as I
receive communion. I wish
the rite's familiar magic
didn't dull my gratitude
for this enormous gift.

I wish I had a closer personal
relationship with Christ,
which I know sounds corny
and alarming. Janet Campbell
gave me a remarkable ikon
the last time I was here;
Christ is in a chair, a throne,
and St. John the Divine,
an androgyne who looks a bit
like Janet, rests his head
upon the Savior's shoulder.
James Madden, priest of Cowley,
dead of cancer earlier
this year at 39, gave her
the image, telling her not to
be afraid to imitate St. John.
There may come a time when
I'm unable to respond with words,
or works, or gratitude to AIDS;
a time when my attitude
caves in, when I'm as weak
as the men who lie across
the dayroom couches hour
after hour, watching sitcoms,
drawing blanks. Maybe
my head will be shaved
and scarred from surgery;
maybe I'll be pencil-
thin and paler than
a ghost, pale as the vesper
light outside my window now.
It would be good to know
that I could close my eyes
and lean my head back
on his shoulder then,
as natural and trusting
as I'd be with a cherished

love. At this moment,
Chris walks in, Christopher
Earl Wiss of Kansas City
and New York, my lover,
my last lover, my first
healthy and enduring relationship
in sobriety, the man
with whom I choose
to share what I have
left of life and time.
This is the hardest
and happiest moment
of the day. G-9
is no place to affirm
a relationship. Two hours
in a chair beside my bed
after eight hours of work
night after night for weeks
. . . it's been a long haul,
and Chris gets tired.
Last week he exploded,
"I hate this, I hate your
being sick and having AIDS
and lying in a hospital
where I can only see you
with a visitor's pass. I hate
that this is going to
get worse." I hate it,
too. We kiss, embrace,
and Chris climbs into bed
beside me, to air-mattress
squeaks. Hold on. We hold on
to each other, to a hope
of how we'll be when I get out.
Let him hold on, please
don't let him lose his
willingness to stick with me,

to make love and to make
love work, to extend
the happiness we've shared.
Please don't let AIDS
make me a monster
or a burden is my prayer.
Too soon, Chris has to leave.
I walk him to the elevator
bank, then totter back
so Raquel can open my I.V.
again. It's not even
mid-evening, but I'm nodding
off. My life's so full, even
(especially?) when I'm here
on G-9. When it's time
to move on to the next step,
that will be a great adventure,
too. Helena Hughes, Tibetan
Buddhist, tells me that
there are three stages in death.
The first is white, like passing
through a thick but porous wall.
The second stage is red;
the third is black, and then
you're finished, ready
for the next event. I'm glad
she has a road map, but I don't
feel the need for one myself.
I've trust enough in all
that's happened in my life,
the unexpected love
and gentleness that rushes in
to fill the arid spaces
in my heart, the way the city
glow fills up the sky
above the river, making it
seem less than night. When

Joe O'Hare flew in last week,
he asked what were the best
times of my New York years;
I said "Today," and meant it.
I hope that death will lift me
by the hair like an angel
in a Hebrew myth, snatch me with
the strength of sleep's embrace,
and gently set me down
where I'm supposed to be,
in just the right place.

Harmony in Red

The woman with the bun
and Roman face
arranges red and yellow
fruit upon a bed
of dark green leaves,
for a centerpiece the colors
of a traffic light, which
hadn't been invented yet
in ought-eight, when all this
popped up in the mind
of an artist — popped
out, rather, in his work.
Arabesques as thick and bluntly
pronged as antlers snake
up the tablecloth and up
the wall behind it, framing
clunky flower baskets
painted in the style of wacky
backgrounds from the *Jiggs
and Maggie* comic strip, though
with a broader brush. Luscious
lemons on the table, purple
sky outside above the lawn
and weird pink barn.
There's a season out there,
spring from the look of it,
and a time of day, less
conclusive. But indoors
the red of walls and tablecloth
and whatever concoction
the decanter holds would
stop time, even if this weren't
an image on a poster
for a show of Impressionist

and Early Modern Paintings
from the U.S.S.R., on the wall
above the table where I drink
my bright red breakfast juice.
Today will be as packed for me
as Matisse's dining room,
with its tasks and patterns.
May I be the woman
with the bun, intent
on lovingly composing
the abundance of the grove
outside or a fruitery
down the street from the studio
in the heart of a city
where the art of the centerpiece
can make a difference still,
as quiet as a nun, serene
as a successful nun
as I pursue my work.

Etiquette in 1969

It was an unfriendly act
to "Bogart," i.e. to
draw deeply on a bomber
as it reached the stage
of roachdom, instead
of passing it along.
A song had been written
about this; Peter Fonda
put it on the soundtrack
of *Easy Rider.* "Nigger-
lipping" was a no-no,
too; it meant to leave
the reefer soggy
with saliva. "Jesus,
Dlugos, you nigger-lipped
the joint!" A hoarse
aggrieved "J'accuse"
behind a barricaded
door in St. Cassian's dorm,
two years before I softly
kissed a black man's lips,
a black dancer's gentle lips,
for the first time.

Radiant Child
for Keith Haring

A baby in a desert
boom town wears a T-shirt
on which is an image
of the Radiant Child.
The infant is no larger
than a young man's hand,
the generous hand of the artist
who died this afternoon.
By the time she's old enough
to crawl like the child
in the drawing, his hand
will wear a coat of dust,
or long ago have been
reduced to ash. Ashleigh
Noelle Snow, my lover's niece,
a brand-new life in a T-shirt
from the Pop Shop, in a snapshot
he would have loved to see.

Swede

Michael Friedman's humorous pet name
for his penis is "The Swede"

I think of this because I'm reading
Michael's new collection of poetry portraits

lots of which are about girls he's known
and loved, especially blondes

and because I have to make
a reservation at the Hotel Suede

in Paris in the next few days
for my boyfriend Chris, a big

Midwestern Swede, and me
Chris would be annoyed I told you that

"I'm an American!" I can hear him say
"Why do people who grow up

in the East identify each other
by their forebears' place of origin?"

so let me correct myself: "a big
Midwestern Swedish-American"

whose forebears came from Norkoping, which sounds
like something people do in Sweden

something useful
and vaguely mysterious

the only real Swede I have ever
known was a girl who smoked cigars

and had a black producer boyfriend
her name was Jonna Bjorkefall

we worked together for a little while
in Washington a long time ago

Jonna's introductions to the mysteries
of America were the stuff of office legend

when she caught the flu and had to see
a doctor, she was asked how she would pay

"I'll stop at the post office on the way
and get a voucher," Jonna declared

another time, she misplaced a huge stack
of checks that public-minded citizens

had sent to help Ralph Nader's work
"Where are those checks?" screeched the boss

and Jonna replied, "Oh, I put them
somewhere," which I and my boyfriend

at the time, an English-American
named Randy Russell, thought was hilarious

though it strikes me just this minute
that both the stories are a lot

more humorous when you throw in
the Swedish accent

my favorite Jonna anecdote
is not a story, but a picture

Jonna and her boyfriend took the Wilson Line
down the Potomac one romantic night

I imagine them, she so blonde,
he so black, watching by the rail

as the city slips away and the darkening
woods of Maryland touch the shore

then Jonna walks alone to the prow,
lights a thin cigar, and contemplates her future

in silhouette against a backlit sky
like the greatest Swede of all,

Greta Garbo, going into exile
at the end of *Queen Christina*

Parachute

The Bergman image of a game
of chess with Death,
though not in a dreamscape
black-and-white as melancholy
films clanking with symbols,
but in a garden in Provence
with goldfish in the fountain
and enormous palms whose topmost
fronds cut into the eternal
blue of sky above the Roman
ruins and the dusty streets
where any door may lead to life's
most perfect meal: that is what
I think of when I remember
I have AIDS. But when
I think of how AIDS kills
my friends, especially
the ones whose paths
through life have least
prepared them to resist
the monster, I think of
an insatiable and prowling beast
with razor teeth and a persistent
stink that sticks to every
living branch or flower
its rank fur brushes
as it stalks its prey.
I think of that disgusting
animal eating my beautiful friends,
innocent as baby deer. Dwight:
so delicate and vain, his spindly
arms and legs pinned down with needles,
pain of tubes and needles, his narrow
chest inflated by machine, his mind

lost in the seven-minute gap
between the respirator's failure
and the time the nurses noticed
something wrong. I wrapped
my limbs around that fragile body
for the first time seven years
ago, in a cheap hotel by the piers,
where every bit of his extravagant
wardrobe — snakeskin boots, skin-tight
pedal pushers in a leopard print,
aviator's scarves, and an electric-
green capacious leather jacket —
lay wrapped in a corner of
his room in a yellow parachute.
It's hard enough to find a parachute
in New York City, I remember thinking,
but finding one the right shade
of canary is the accomplishment
of the sort of citizen with whom
I wish to populate my life.
Dwight the dancer, Dwight the fashion
illustrator and the fashion plate,
Dwight the child, the borderline
transvestite, Dwight the frightened,
infuriating me because an anti-AZT
diatribe by some eccentric
in a rag convinced him not to take
the pills with which he might
still be alive, Dwight
on the runway, Dwight on the phone
suggesting we could still have sex
if we wore "raincoats," Dwight
screwing a girl from Massapequa
in the ladies' room at Danceteria
(he wore more makeup and had better
jewelry than she did), Dwight planning
the trip to London or Berlin where he

would be discovered and his life
transformed. Dwight erased,
evicted from his own young body.
Dwight dead. At Bellevue, I wrapped
my arms around his second skin
of gauze and scars and tubing,
brushed my hand against
his plats, and said goodbye.
I hope I'm not the one
who loosed the devouring animal
that massacred you, gentle boy.
You didn't have a clue
to how you might stave off
the beast. I feel so confident
most days that I can stay
alive, survive and thrive
with AIDS. But when I see
Dwight smile and hear his fey
delighted voice inside my head,
I know AIDS is no chess game
but a hunt, and there is no
way of escaping the bloody
horror of the kill, no way
to bail out, no bright
parachute beside my bed.

Turandot

When I try to imagine
what heaven will be like,
I think of Puccini's Pekinese
court, ruled by a big Joan Sutherland
type wearing an enormous headdress,
where riddling has metastasized
from a show of wit into a burning
passion, consuming all the time
that passes in the progress
toward an end that never comes,
and everyone, not only the sympathetic
slightly ridiculous Ping, Pang and Pong,
has long since been sated by the marvels
of the capital, and just wants to go home.

D.O.A.

"You knew who I was
when I walked in the door.
You thought that I was dead.
Well, I am dead. A man
can walk and talk and even
breathe and still be dead."
Edmond O'Brien is perspiring
and chewing up the scenery
in my favorite film noir,
D.O.A. I can't stop watching,
can't stop relating. When I walked down
Columbus to Endicott last night
to pick up Tor's new novel,
I felt the eyes of every
Puerto Rican teen, crackhead,
yuppie couple focus on my cane
and makeup. "You're dead,"
they seemed to say in chorus.
Somewhere in a dark bar
years ago, I picked up "luminous
poisoning." My eyes glowed
as I sipped my drink. After that,
there was no cure, no turning back.
I had to find out what was gnawing
at my gut. The hardest part's
not even the physical effects:
stumbling like a drunk (Edmond
O'Brien was one of Hollywood's
most active lushes) through
Forties sets, alternating sweats
and fevers, reptilian spots
on face and scalp. It's having
to say goodbye like the scene
where soundtrack violins go crazy

as O'Brien gives his last embrace
to his girlfriend-*cum*-Girl
Friday, Paula, played by Pamela
Britton. They're filmdom's least
likely lovers — the squat and jowly
alkie and the homely fundamentally
talentless actress who would hit
the height of her fame as the pillhead-
acting landlady on *My Favorite Martian*
fifteen years in the future. I don't have
fifteen years, and neither does Edmond
O'Brien. He has just enough time to tell
Paula how much he loves her, then
to drive off in a convertible
for the showdown with his killer.
I'd like to have a showdown too, if I
could figure out which pistol-packing
brilliantined and ruthless villain
in a hound's-tooth overcoat took
my life. Lust, addiction, being
in the wrong place at the wrong
time? That's not the whole
story. Absolute fidelity
to the truth of what I felt, open
to the moment, and in every case
a kind of love: all of the above
brought me to this tottering
self-conscious state — pneumonia,
emaciation, grisly cancer,
no future, heart of gold,
passionate engagement with a great
B film, a glorious summer
afternoon in which to pick up
the ripest plum tomatoes of the year
and prosciutto for the feast I'll cook
tonight for the man I love,
phone calls from my friends

and a walk to the park, ignoring
stares, to clear my head. A day
like any, like no other. Not so bad
for the dead.

Serpent's Tail

1986 to 1996

TEN YEARS WITH ATTITUDE!

"If you've got hold of a book that doesn't fit the categories
and doesn't miss them either,
the chances are that you've got a serpent by the tail."

ADAM MARS-JONES

"The Serpent's Tail boldly goes
where no reptile has gone before ... More power to it!"

MARGARET ATWOOD

you would like to receive a catalogue of our current publications please write to:

FREEPOST, Serpent's Tail,
4 Blackstock Mews, LONDON N4 2BR

(No stamp necessary if your letter is posted in the United Kingdom.)